MATED *to the*
ENFORCER

Portal City Protectors Book 2

GEORGETTE ST CLAIR
LETEISHA NEWTON

Beyond DEF
https://www.beyonddeflit.com

Editing – Tiffany Fox and C.A. Houghton; Beyond DEF
Cover design – LeTeisha Newton; Beyond DEF
Interior Layout & eBook Adaptation: Deena Rae Schoenfeldt; E-Book Builders for Beyond DEF

File version: 201910012.010

BOOKS BY GEORGETTE

Shifters of Silver Peak

Mate Marked
Mate for a Month
A Very Shifty Christmas

Tri-Valley Dragon

Bride of the Dragon
Love Burns

Twin Alphas

Claimed
Desired

Neck Deep

Neck Deep in Trouble
Neck Deep in Vampires

Curvy Girls

The Big Girl and the Bounty
Hunter
Sweet Surrender
Claimed by the Cowboy

Standalones

I Married a Warlock
Like Cats and Dogs
Lion's Den
The Dragon's Christmas Wish
Shifter's Solace
Furrever Yours

BOOKS BY LETEISHA

Dark Romance

Pinnacle Heirs
(co-authored with Ginger Talbot)

Irrepairable
Cutter
Mangled

The Lost Series

One Hour Girl
Scarred
Phenomenal

Standalones

Whispers in the Dark
Going Under
Vanquished

Paranormal Romance

Portal City Protectors
(co-authored with Georgette St Clair)

Mated to the Capo - St. Clair Only
Mated to the Enforcer
Mated to the Prince
Fated to the Traitor

Single Titles

Claimed Trilogy
Taken Trilogy

e

Military Romance

A SEALed Fate Series

Protecting Butterfly
Protecting Goddess
Protecting Vixen
Protecting Hawk
Protecting Heartbeat
Corporate Hitman Trilogy

MATED TO THE *ENFORCER*

The lions want to kill her … and then it gets worse …

Staying under the radar of the Mage Society's Trinity Council hasn't been much of an issue for bakery owner Kalinda Thorton, but when her supposedly weak magical powers start causing afternoon delights, she knows she's in trouble. Add in one dangerously alluring wolf who says he wants to eat more than just her confections and life in Encantado, Nevada, has gone from enchanted to cursed in one afternoon.

He'll huff and puff and keep his mate safe …

Kalinda belongs to the big bad wolf—Romano Moretti. He'll stop at nothing to protect his mate, even if she doesn't yet know they belong together. But clashing with the Trinity Council and a pride of lion shifters at the same time is a lot of work for one wolf, and he might have bitten off more than he can chew.

Kalinda is nobody's witch …

Screw the Council, screw the lions, and most especially screw Romano's scorching touch and fierce protection. She'll handle things on her own even if it kills her, except Romano's sizzling embrace makes her yearn for things she's never thought she wanted. She's beginning to wonder if a big bad wolf is exactly the kind of ally she needs, in more ways than one.

With the fate of the town at stake, Kalinda will need to trust someone … or everyone is doomed.

MATED *to the* ENFORCER

CHAPTER ONE

"**N**ot now," Kalinda Thorton muttered under her breath. "Anytime but now."

Her magic was a fickle bitch. Weak and barely noticeable most of her life, it had been flaring up explosively for the last few months at the worst possible moments. She felt the weird, prickly energy that warned her the strength of her magic was shooting through the roof for no logical reason, which meant her coordination would be wobbly and spills were a serious risk.

She smoothed down her black tuxedo jacket over her black skirt and slowly counted to ten. When that didn't work, she rubbed the tingling spot over her heart and took a deep breath. Kalinda had been dealing with aggravating heart palpitations, tingling, and weird bursts of her normally less-than-stellar magical ability.

Running Kalinda's Katering in Encantado, Nevada, was a headache to begin with. Portal cities weren't all glitz and glamour like the outside world believed. Battles, attacks, and paying for protection all ran rampant in the city of sin.

Kalinda stood straight and, by sheer effort of will, forced her hands to stop trembling. *Just a couple of hours and then on to the next client, K. You've got this.*

Kalinda stopped long enough to check her braid wasn't out of place in the mirror then went on her way to check on her guests. Rock Landing was *the* place for Viscount Pride parties, and she'd served here often enough to have the layout memorized.

One platter, a delicious Thai noodle in spicy peanut sauce, was left to the side, and she grabbed it, stifling the urge to fuss. The Leo of the Viscount Pride shouldn't have been left waiting to be served.

"Table two is looking for another helping. Get it done," Silva called, her short legs already carrying her away and out of the preparation area as the other servers plated her requests. Kalinda grabbed it, happy at least one of her girls was moving and getting stuff done.

"I've got table two. Keep going with the rest," Kalinda ordered and headed out.

A loud buzz of conversation thrummed in her ears. The pride was rowdy. Some were eating, while others mingled and joked, and a pair of lionesses circled each other readying to start a mock fight over a plate of steak tartare between them.

What is it with cats and playing with their food?

Kalinda danced around them, setting table two's plate down with a flourish. "Enjoy!"

The young cub at the table growled his thanks, and she continued on her way.

Okaaaaaaaaaaay.

The Leo, Orion Viscount, sat in a throne-like chair, wrapped in a custom-cut tan suit that did nothing but blend with the blond mane around his shoulders. The thick waves were shaggy and rough, just like the animal that lived within him, and his rounded ears stuck out. He surveyed the happenings around him from his elevated perch, a single round table in front of him and a female at his side. Kalinda thought they called their enforcers "chargers."

Built like an Amazon, and a head taller than Kalinda's own six feet, the charger turned her golden eyes on Kalinda and sniffed the air before nodding her head imperceptibly to continue. Prides tended to have a male at the head, with a few other males in positions of rank, but were mostly dominated by women.

Half the damn cubs here are probably the Leo's.

Orion Viscount drank his wine from an enormous glass and pretended he was too important to acknowledge Kalinda's approach. Whatever. His disdain didn't bother her. As her mother would have said: "*Consider the source.*"

Orion's eyes coldly swept the room as if he were thinking, "I pity you peons for not being able to sneeze on money and flush it down the toilet. Bwahahaha!"

"Your meal is served, Leo. I wanted to bring it personally and thank you for your continued use of Kalinda's Katering. If there is anything else, don't hesitate to ask."

Was that sarcasm? Nah, only in her head.

He finally turned his head and sniffed the air. "Your service is appalling, and your magic fouls the air, *mage*."

And you're about two seconds from having my stiletto in your eye, pussy cat.

Kalinda smiled sweetly. "Enjoy!"

She was not going to respond to him the way he deserved just because it would make her temporarily feel better. Any trouble she caused would rile up his pride and put her employees in danger, and her prime job was to protect her girls. Sure, they might have to deal with an occasional groping shifter or touchy daywalker, but she'd taught her girls how to handle them too.

A well-placed foot or elbow helped a lot of that.

Her cheeks were hurting from smiling so hard, and she turned to leave, but a sudden screech stopped her in her tracks. The room became deafeningly silent as she spun around.

"You've killed me."

The Leo's deep voice had suddenly gone high-pitched and whiny. She blinked for a few seconds, wondering exactly how the Leo had attained *that* level of octave before she snapped back reality.

"What? Are you okay?" Kalinda's heart raced.

He fanned himself and yanked at his tie, his face turning red as a tomato. Kalinda counted at least three large veins popping out on his forehead. His charger gripped his shoulders, keeping him upright as she growled at Kalinda.

What was going on?

"She's poisoned me!" Leo wheezed.

Kalinda shook her head. "I've done no such thing. What are you talking about?"

Orion jerked, his mouth opening and closing like a fish out of water before he slumped over dramatically. "Dead. I'm dead."

She would have laughed at the picture in front of her if she wasn't surrounded by pissed-off lions and lionesses with her staff's lives in the balance. Heat spread through her limbs, a sign her magic was about to pop a filter.

Great. Just great.

"Mr. Viscount, the meal was cooked and delivered just as you ordered. Your charger sniffed for anything out of the ordinary. If you need the assistance of Warlock Cyrus, he can be called immediately."

They were *shifters*. There was no way any ingredient in the food would have made it past their noses.

Kalinda turned and snapped her fingers at her girls, hoping they'd get the signal and go. Silva, her white hair pulled into a messy bun atop her head was the smallest of them all, her delicate pointy ears a sign of her Fae ancestry. But she was quick, darting between the shifters to each girl and yanking them behind her.

"I'll call Cyrus right away," Silva announced.

I'm giving that girl a raise.

The heat in Kalinda's body built, hotter and hotter, spiraling from her heart and out through her fingertips. Without thinking, she touched Orion, spreading magic to him as well.

Calm. Be calm and talk to me.

His eyes glazed over, and he smiled.

Orion started wheezing again and spluttered, "P-pretty. Such … dark … skin. Y-you're g-gorgeous. You want to be my Nubian princess?"

Whaaaat? No, he didn't. Seriously? Did he just go there?

Okay, that wasn't what she'd expected to happen.

"Thank you," she said with a tight-lipped smile. "Now, what's wrong with your food?"

"I could make you Prima."

As in the head female of a Pride? Um, no thank you.

She flashed him her most diplomatic smile. "I appreciate the offer. But first, let's talk about what's wrong, okay?"

"Remove your hands from the Leo!" The charger—what was her name? Oh, Roxi—jumped between Kalinda and Orion, breaking the connection. He immediately went back into spasms, flopping down to the ground and screaming again.

"You've poisoned me! I can't breathe. I'm dying. Can't you see I'm dying?"

If you can talk, you can breathe. Melodramatic much?

Dang it, she wasn't supposed to be thinking like that. She took a deep breath and backed away from Roxi with her palms up in a placating gesture.

"I just wanted to make sure he was all right and see what the issue is. He ordered the Thai noodle in peanut sa—"

"*Peanuts.*"

Kalinda's ears were bleeding, she knew it, and she knew she heard several glasses shatter from Mr. Leo's newest interpretation of Minnie Riperton's skillset. Hitting high notes like that really should have crushed his vocal cords.

Hand to his chest, head screwed sideways, and his muzzle twisted up in the greatest affront, Outraged, Orion must have forgotten about not being able to breathe as he huffed at her, outraged.

"Just because you are friends with the Lombardi Pack Alpha bitch doesn't mean you are untouchable," Roxi hissed through a steadily morphing face.

"I didn't poison him!" she protested. "I gave him what he ordered."

"The Leo is allergic to peanuts. He never would have ordered it."

"I can show you the paperwork. Have someone follow me to my office. I'll prove it."

Was she terrified? Of course, but she didn't run a business in one of the most dangerous places in the world and maintain Level-7 wards on her windows in case of attack to back down at every challenge. Shifters were the worst with dominance and only understood things when they got knocked over the head.

She always knew she was on her own when it came to handling emergencies. In theory, the Mage Council provided protection, but they only came down for major squabbles between groups; they wouldn't waste their time on an issue like this. They'd rather let the pride get rid of her and be done with it.

Roxi nodded at someone behind Kalinda. "Take her, and kill her if the information is wrong."

Wonderful.

Kalinda turned on her heels, head held high, back straight, and floated. Her mother always told her a woman had to fight the whole world, and the best way to do it was with a smile, good character, and a hell of a walk.

She ignored the snapping shifters with each step and avoided the large beige lioness circle on the edge—they'd already shifted and were ready to attack. Kalinda put one foot in front of the other, hips swaying, and never looked anywhere but between the shoulder blades of the charger escorting her back into the serving room.

As they entered, Orion let out another piercing wail, and Kalinda grimaced.

"What room did you set up as your office?" the no-name-charger sneered at Kalinda. Her blond hair was cut close to the scalp, shoulders barely contained in her sleek mermaid style dress, and blood-red nails curled like claws.

"The Cub Area."

They had never let her into the inner sanctum of Rock Landing, instead keeping her to the children's space just off the kitchen and open ballroom. Kalinda was escorted into her makeshift office and went right to her papers. She found what she needed in one shuffle before handing it over.

"Here is the order list, signed and confirmed."

"We shall see."

Someone had their panties in a bunch.

What would Kalinda have to gain by killing Orion? If this was a plan to extort her, she'd find out who was behind it. There was no way in hell she was going to let her business reputation be destroyed by someone playing a game.

She was proud of how she'd managed to build up one of the most sought-after catering businesses from scratch after being forced to move to Encantado. And nobody would take that away from her.

Her magic, low as it was, had come to light while she was in culinary school. Luckily, she'd managed to graduate before the Federal Bureau of Magical Containment swept her out of her life and into a portal city.

Her dreams of owning a five-star restaurant in the Bay Area disappeared. Her fiancé had chosen not to come with her; he didn't want his children tainted by having "magic blood." She'd clawed her way to where she was now in Encantado, despite the loss of her mother a few years back, and she'd made it her mission to make Kalinda's a household name.

"It seems in order. Are there any other copies? A way you manipulated this receipt?"

"The signing isn't done until we get here, as always, and I have no access to a system here. Roxi signed off on the menu, as you can see. Please take up any discrepancies with her."

"Are you calling our head charger a traitor?"

Did. She. Just. Spit. On. Me?

"No, I'm saying Kalinda's Katering has done what was ordered and will be happy to serve another meal, if that's what you would prefer."

Suddenly, Kalinda began to sweat and breathe hard, as if she'd been transported into a sauna. Hot. It was so freaking hot. Her magic, which normally did nothing more than make her food more delicious and add a sense of comfort, pulsed under her skin. She resisted the urge to rake at her arms, but she couldn't stop the magic from leaking out. Finally, brilliant rays of gold and white spread from her, weaving its way around the charger in front of her and back out the door.

The charger dropped to the floor, purring, stretching her back, and kneading at the floor. Sharp nails curved from her fingertips and plucked at the rug. Kalinda took a step back, eyeing her suspiciously.

"Um, Kalinda? You may want to come out here," Silva called.

Kalinda stepped over the lioness currently humping the air in the middle of the floor and headed out into the prep area.

The room had gone crazy.

Silva, who had a knack for canceling magic not Fae based, was the only one standing. Literally. Kalinda's servers rolled on the floor, laughing and singing random songs, while the party outside had turned into Woodstock.

"What the hell?" Kalinda blinked hard and shook her head. Nope, not having an illusion. Gold and white ribbons danced over everyone, slipping over even Roxi and Orion, until the Leo had the aforementioned charger bent over the table and—

"All right, time to get out of here. Do you see the colors?"

Silva frowned at Kalinda. "What colors?"

"The gold and white lights. You don't see them?"

"Maybe a drug was filtered into the ventilation and you're affected too. I think we should all leave."

Kalinda shook her head, confused. She wasn't crazy—the magic flowing from her was in color and had caused everyone in the room to get frisky. Even the few cubs who'd been in attendance were outside, racing up and down a jungle gym Kalinda could see through a large bay window.

With shaking hands and a pounding heart, Kalinda did what she did best—direct.

Looking to her cooks and servers, she pointed to the front door. "Get out of here, now. There are vans waiting outside."

"But—"

"Don't argue. I'll meet you back at the shop." She would stay on scene and get what help she could. She couldn't just leave the Pride here in this state, especially knowing she'd probably caused it.

Kalinda was going to have to call her best friend Zoey and her mate Dominic. The Lombardi Pack was feared and respected throughout Encantado, and whatever was happening here, they'd be able to handle it.

She hoped. Of course, the price would be high—Zoey was going to give her grief for the rest of her life, and probably into the afterlife.

She knew it, but she picked up her spell phone and dialed anyway.

"Kalinda? Everything okay?"

"Well, that depends. I mean, it's only like I may have used magic to turn Rock Landing into a massive orgy after being accused of attempting to kill the Leo. I may have started an incident. Other than that, everything is peachy."

"You *what?*" Zoey squawked.

"Just come help me. Whenever this stuff calms down, they're probably going to want to kill me. I'd like to stay alive today."

"You're going to have to explain this better when we get there."

"Who are you bringing?" Kalinda felt a sudden flutter of alarm. "Not him. Don't say you're bringing him."

Zoey actually laughed, the wench. "Romano isn't going to pass up a chance to see this, not in a million years."

Ugh. Not Romano! The Lombardi Pack's enforcer was far too arrogant, far too sexy for his own good—or hers, for that matter—and he was a total flirt. When he walked down the street, you could practically see women's panties melting. Well, that wouldn't happen with Kalinda. Not today, not ever. She'd already gone down the love 'em and get screwed over train. She wasn't interested in a second trip.

"You don't actually have to tell him about it," she argued.

"I have to tell my mate, and he tells Romano everything," Zoey protested with a laugh.

"Seriously?" Kalinda groaned. "I never should have warned you when the *Capo* came to claim you!"

"Ha! That's what friends are for, silly. That and having each other's backs. I've got yours."

A wave of dizziness rolled over Kalinda, and black spots swam in front of her eyes. She was going to fall and mess up her uniform. She *hated* being dirty. "Oh, that's good because I think I'm going to pass out."

Zoey's worried voice was very far away now. "Kalinda? Ka—"

Yep. Dry cleaning won't be getting these stains out.

CHAPTER *Two*

"**C**ome on, buttercup. As much as I'd like to see you falling at my feet, I'd much rather it be done *because* of me."

The world was hard, warm, and smelled of deep woods. It was a … comforting scent. Kalinda had never really thought of the woods as comforting, but right now, in this darkness, her body drained and her mind going haywire, she clung to it. She curled her fingers into silken earth, scrunching her face when dirt didn't crumble between her fingers. But even that thought shattered as quickly as it came. She held on to the anchor, pulling it closer, inhaling deeply.

Darkness gave way to fire, burning and sizzling along her skin. The sky was dark, pitched with billowing smoke, and an acrid taste lined the back of her throat. She hated it. A failure. A loss. Tears welled up in her eyes. Here, on this land, lost to the blue-purple blaze of the dragon, she'd failed to save any of them.

"Hey, baby. We're here. It's okay."

That same voice again, baritone and rumbly. That wasn't right. She *felt* it even before she heard the words. The ground vibrated under her with each sound. She liked the way it soothed the charred edges of her nerves.

A warm thumb caressed her cheek and she—
Thumb?

Kalinda jerked awake, groaning when she knocked forehead first into the most annoying man she'd met in her life.

"Don't touch me," she warned.

"Well, hello to you too, sunshine. And warn me *after* you detach yourself from clinging. Or you could stay right where you are. I'd prefer that option."

In three seconds, she realized where she was and what was going on. She also realized a few other things. One, she was outside of Rock Landing with the gold and white lights all gone. Two, Zoey grinned at her like a loon, rubbing her rounded belly at the side of a massive white wolf—Dominic, her mate and the *Capo di tutti Capi* of the Lombardi Pack. Three—and this one really annoyed her—she was in the arms of his scarred *Capo*, Romano. He held her off the ground as if she weighed nothing, and he wore the same grin he always did when he saw her.

Oh, and lastly, he was absolutely correct. She had her arms wrapped around him, her fingers twisted into the material of his suit jacket over his back, like a vine. Woohoo! That's just brilliant. Embarrassed and face flaming, she detached herself and waited for him to put her down.

She should have known better.

Instead, he cocked his head to the side for a moment and watched her, his ever-present smile plastered on his face. His grin pulled his scars tight, nearly white on his face. Romano was a gorgeous man, there was no denying that. He was taller than her, and that said a lot at her height, with dark hair and swarthy skin. As Dominic's enforcer and a warrior-class wolf, he was built as big as an oak tree. Most striking of all was the multitude of scars up one side of his face. They didn't detract from his looks at all. Instead, they enhanced them, giving him an edge of danger and power she couldn't help but notice.

The panty-melting kind.

As if reading her mind, his nostrils flared and he took a sniff before his smile widened.

"Anytime, beautiful. Anytime."

Kalinda rolled her eyes. She hated that word. She wasn't the type to be beautiful and not recognize it or not like being acknowledged. She'd been courted to be a model for most of her life before they found out she was a mage and kicked her out of human society. But what bothered her was it was *all* people saw first. Not her skill level, the pain of losing her mother, her work ethic, or her need to care for others. No, they saw a trophy, and she'd be that for no one.

"Lines are annoying and uncouth. Put me down, please."

Romano opened his mouth to say something, but the doors to Rock Landing burst open behind her and Roxi and two other lionesses rushed out. Romano's demeanor shifted, all smiles and laughter gone in an instant before he lowered Kalinda to her feet and pushed her behind him. She'd never seen him so serious.

"We want the mage. She attempted to kill our Leo. And she spelled us. The penalty is death."

Romano … rippled. She didn't know how else to describe it. The air around him stilled as his skin rolled for a moment, black fur flashing for an instant.

"You will watch your mouth when you speak about her."

The lioness hissed. "It's our right."

Kalinda stepped around Romano to address Roxi. He stepped with her but allowed her to be partially seen. "I already proved the meal was signed for and was given as ordered. Besides, how could I have given your Leo something he's allergic to without your wonderful nose picking up on it?"

"I would have to agree," Romano added.

No, she didn't feel warm and fuzzy at his support of her *at all*. *People say they have your back, but it never lasts, does it Kalinda?*

"We haven't finished investigating yet, and that doesn't address the fact you used your magic on us. Come with us, mage."

"It seems you're hard of hearing," Zoey spoke up. "She is under the protection of Dominic Lombardi of the Lombardi Pack. And she would have no reason to use her magic on you, so clearly, there's another explanation. If you must see her, schedule a meet on neutral territory, and we'll sit down and talk like the civilized animals we are."

"You do not speak for the Alpha."

Okay, Roxi was either fearless or stupid. Instantly, the white wolf shifted into a very naked, very pissed off Dominic.

"*Down.*"

The power of his magic pulsed out to everyone around the room. Romano whimpered but succeeded in staying on his feet.

Zoey fared better, burying her face for a moment in Dominic's arm before looking ahead again.

The lionesses? They were pissed off but couldn't react. All three struggled to stay on their knees at this point, hissing and spitting at Dominic. They all sounded like very large, *very* angry cats ready to fight. While she didn't know much, Kalinda had been told by Zoey that an Alpha male could make other shifters bow under the power of their Alpha status. It also extended to other shifter types, to a point. Dominic had grown stronger taking over as an Alpha, and his power showed.

Roxi recovered the best, getting to a crouch but no longer hissing. "She won't be allowed to get away with this. We will plan that meet, and we will see *you* later."

The last was directed at Kalinda, and she felt the threat down to her toes. And for what? She'd proven she hadn't poisoned the Leo. And, as Orion stepped out of the building as well, he didn't look any worse for wear.

If Orion thought his presence as Leo was going to change anything, he had another think coming. More wolves pulled up and stepped out of cars instantly.

Orion lifted placating hands. "We just want her, Dominic. We don't want war."

"And I'm making it clear that touching her *would* be war. Send a message when you want to meet, but we are leaving," Dominic ordered.

"Come on, Kalinda," Romano added.

What was going on? None of this made sense. They shouldn't be this ready to tear her down. She was a caterer, for God's sake. Sure, if Orion were allergic to peanuts, feeding him some would have been treacherous, but one of the lionesses had already seen that wasn't the case from the evidence, and tainted food should never had gotten through. This had to be more than about the food, but Kalinda couldn't figure out what.

Romano wrapped his arm around her, pulling her close. "There won't be a later. You'll be staying. Dominic, I'll keep her within the compound."

She fought against Romano's restraining arm, but he didn't let her go. "You can't do that. I have a business to run. This has all been some big misunderstanding. Let's just have the meeting and get this cleared up."

"I'm upset you don't want to spend quality time with me, sweetheart, but now isn't the time for debate."

Once again, she was in Romano's arms, and he was moving quickly toward the cars, apparently with her as his baby bundle. Zoey and Dominic piled in after them.

"What spell are they talking about?"

Leave it to Zoey to get to the quick of the situation. Bless the woman.

"I'm not sure, really. And the peanut allergy thing doesn't make any sense. Is it a ruse?"

"Silva called us and told us you were seeing gold and white," Dominic explained.

Ah, that explained why they're asking. Note to self: don't give Silva that raise.

Kalinda shrugged, still on baby status and sitting in Romano's lap. She shifted to signal wanting to get up, but he only smiled and wrapped her tighter. So … not going anywhere. Got it. She should have fought harder, but she was still feeling weak and shaky from whatever craziness had happened earlier.

Yeah, that's why she wasn't fighting to get away.

"Well, you know, Zoey, how I've been talking to you about how my magic has been weird?"

Zoey nodded. "Yeah. And you smell different right now."

Kalinda hadn't thought about that. Dominic had bitten Zoey, and with everything that had happened, Kalinda hadn't thought about whether Zoey's senses or powers had changed.

"The medicine didn't work?"

"Not exactly. I'll explain later." She looked to Dominic for a moment, and he smiled softly, rubbing her stomach.

It was odd seeing the man they'd all thought of as a murderous leech looking soft and sweet, but there was nothing but love when he looked at Zoey.

"For now, we need to know why your scent has changed," Dominic added. "Tell us about the colors."

"I don't know how to explain it, really. My magic has always been low-level, at most geared to adding a sense of comfort to my food. I can't control elements or anything like that."

"But the wards on your building are Level 7. What level are you as a mage?"

"I pay for those, to be honest. It's a nice chunk of change out of the profits, but it keeps us all safe."

Zoey smiled. "And we love you for it."

"Love you too, girl. Most of the time. Except when you're so ... happy. Which is most of the time." Zoey pretended to look hurt, but Kalinda ignored her. "Anyway, my magic has been funny since the portals have been opening up. Sometimes, it's stronger than normal and flaring at odd times. Today, I panicked when they were all set to attack and I sent out calming vibes, but it happened during a time when my magic was flaring. Apparently, it pushed out gold and white lights from me, and everyone it touched got ... um ... frisky."

Dominic blinked. "Say again?"

"I may or may not have started an orgy." Kalinda cringed. That sucked even saying it.

"Remember when I first met you and threatened to eat you? That could still happen." Romano's voice was a sexy growl. "I'd like to join in on that action."

Kalinda thought about slapping Romano again, but the last time she'd done that it only left her with a hurt hand and him stating it tickled. This time, she glared at him, ignoring how her panties wanted to melt—again.

The things must have been produced with edible material instead of fabric.

Romano leaned in, his hot breath sliding over her neck, and her pulse jumped. If she thought she was hot when her magic flared before, she was ready to ignite now. That easy. Just being in his arms and having his mouth so close to her skin was all it took for her to lose part of her brain capacity.

"I think you like that idea more than you want to show," he whispered against her flesh.

No. Yes. Maybe?

Kalinda knew his type; they were all the same in the portal cities and in the world of normal humans. Men who flirted, who always joked ... The women who took them up on it were just another notch in their belts. She had too much going on to be simply another go in the bed. It didn't matter how sexy he was, she wasn't one for games. She couldn't take him seriously. What she could be, however, was annoyed with herself and her reaction to his obviously insincere flirtation.

"I can still try to kick you where the sun don't shine. It would hurt, but it's worth a shot," she warned.

He chuckled, the sound rumbling deep within his chest. She only felt it because she was so close, not because it made her lady parts wet.

Right.

Dominic sighed. "Pipe down, children."

"He started it!" Kalinda argued.

"Look, he jokes, a lot, but there is no better man when it comes to protecting my family, and with how Zoey feels about you, you're family."

Kalinda didn't know how to respond to that, not really. She'd lost access to her family coming to the portal city, like many other mages caught up in the sweep. It made her feel … something she couldn't quite examine immediately.

"Can we focus on the matter at hand? I think they wanted to kill me."

"No, I think they wanted to *take* you, and that means they want something from you. Something we don't know about, and I want to know why. The allergy thing was just a ruse to start something, but the question is *what* made them interested in you in the first place?" Dominic answered.

"I'm not inclined to call the Council in to find out. We saw what happened last time we dealt with them. We don't know who's trustworthy and who's not," Romano argued.

Dominic shrugged. "Then we use Zahara."

Zoey sat up straight, excitement bubbling from her. "The witch doctor?"

"Why are you so excited?" Kalinda wondered if they were all crazy. *She* was the one in danger.

Zoey shrugged. "Haven't really had a chance to meet her. I'd go for a chance to see what she can tell us."

Zahara typically only worked with those who had enough money to afford her services. It wasn't because she charged high for snake oil but because she was the real deal. From what Kalinda had heard, she was invited to join the Council of Mages but turned it down because of too many restrictions on her actions. She wanted to be able to freely use her gifts as she saw fit.

So Zahara opened her practice in District 12, and many of the daywalkers had her to thank for being able to walk around in the sun for a period of time. She'd been the mastermind behind the concoction that helped them. The Council of Mages left her alone as long as she didn't try anything against them. Kalinda didn't know if Zahara had ever tried, as there wasn't much more than that known about her, but Kalinda knew this: anyone the Council had to make an agreement with was powerful.

Dominic shifted in his seat and looked at Romano. "For now, Romano, keep Kalinda with you and don't leave her. If she must travel to work, you go with her and don't let her out of your sight. She's kept safe until we understand what's going on and why the Viscount Pride put on a show to take her."

Kalinda snapped her fingers. "Hello? I'm right here. You can ask me how that may get in my way. I'm sure there are other wolves you can appoint. I'd like to be able to go home."

"Aw, you shouldn't have. I'd love to see your home. I could have my things moved in today."

Kalinda ignored Romano and kept looking at Dominic. "Alpha?"

Dominic sighed. "Besides me, Romano is the strongest wolf of the Lombardi Pack. I can't leave my mate unprotected, and I can't in good conscience have danger so close to her when our child is in her womb. I'm giving you my right hand in order to keep you safe. Pack lands will ensure other enforcers are there and the pride won't come there. Your home is a different story."

"And any other wolf would find themselves looking for their teeth. But I mean, hey, go ahead and let the youth die for beauty."

Kalinda tried, she really did, to ignore Romano's added quip, but she couldn't help it. She stomped down on his instep, hard. He howled, and she smiled cruelly at him. "Don't play with me or try to rearrange my life."

As it did earlier, his face lost all manner of joking. "And don't think I'd allow you to ever be hurt or give your protection over to another." He glared at her, his dark eyes piercing.

Kalinda sucked in a breath, believing him. But what would that mean for her? She had to keep her work going, and Romano was a distraction she didn't need.

Okay, so she could admit, at least to herself, having such a powerful, sexy man around wouldn't be the worst thing to ever happen, but she didn't want him to assume he'd have more than just access to her for protection. She wasn't going to lose who she was.

She loved Zoey, independent and happy soul that she was, but she hadn't run a business and claimed a place in the world. Kalinda's Katering had partnered with The Daily Grind, a coffee shop in the district, to sell her baked goods and to also have their coffee as part of her events. If things kept going the way they were, their partnership could go national and she'd have to be available to travel for that if she could.

She had dreams, chances, things to conquer … She didn't want to feel, once again, like her life was changing by no choice of her own because someone else saw something in her. She refused.

"It's me or me. Or, or me. Take your pick, then I'll tell you what each one gives you."

Kalinda didn't care how good he looked—and he looked really good. She wasn't going to just take him up on his offer. She liked her own path. "And what if I choose option number four?"

Romano arched a brow. "What option would that be?"

"Staying on pack grounds and *not* having you as a personal escort." *Boom!* Kalinda thought that was an *ah-mazing* idea.

Instead of responding to her directly, Romano tossed a pointed look Zoey's way. "I didn't take your old boss to be a scaredy cat, Zoey, but maybe I was wrong."

What did he just call me? Oh no.

Kalinda shifted in his lap enough so she could semi-face him and dug her nails into his collarbone. Romano winced but otherwise made no outward show of what she was doing. She leaned in, ignoring his smile and his scent to whisper in his ear.

"Don't try to handle me. You won't like my retaliation."

Romano wrapped his arms around her, fisting one giant hand in her braid and forcing her head into the crook of his neck. She melded to him, chest to chest, her butt pressed firmly to his rapidly hardening front.

"Oh, Kalinda, I think you've wanted to be managed for a very long time; you just haven't found someone strong enough to do it. So you get all three of me."

Three? Oh, the options. Right.

"And you know what that means? By the end of this all, you'll know *exactly* who you belong to."

Hell. No.

But part of her, deep inside, was boiling-hot and turned on. A part of her she couldn't deny wanted to say *yes.*

CHAPTER *THREE*

Kalinda Thorton was unlike any woman Romano had ever met, within the pack or outside of it. She was strong, and that was saying a lot with the women they had in the pack. She wasn't going to be anyone's doormat, and she didn't care he was a shifter when she threatened him.

He could get behind a woman like that—permanently. And on top of, and any other position she'd care to explore.

Of course, said occupant of his thoughts would rather leave him hanging out to dry than accept the desire pulsing between them. And it was. She could deny it all she liked, but his wolf senses still picked it up. The moment she was around him, his wolf wanted to start a firework party with Kalinda as the star—on her hands and knees.

To be honest, Romano did wonder *why* his wolf reacted so heavily to her.

He was tempted to shift near her to see how his wolf reacted, but if he learned anything from watching Dominic, it was that having a mate chosen before she even had a chance to understand could cause a ton of issues.

Granted, if things called for it, that's exactly what Romano would do.

Of course, he could be jumping the gun with all of this, but he doubted it. For whatever the reason or cause, Kalinda was *his*, and he'd make sure she knew it.

For now, she stood in the middle of his home fit to cause a tornado right in his living room. He smiled at her just because he couldn't keep it at bay and he knew it riled her up.

"It's been *four hours*. Four. How are my things in your house? Why are they here?"

He could probably explain he'd thought to make her comfortable by having some of her own items in a new space during a dangerous situation, but instead …

"Why not?"

If a woman could scream silently, Kalinda did.

She warmed up the space, filled it. He'd never been one for a lot of things to clutter the space. He'd kept his living room to a simple couch and recliner in the same matching chocolate and his large flat screen mounted to the wall. The kitchen, though stocked with stainless steel appliances and an island, wasn't used very often.

His bedroom got all the attention, but he doubted she'd like to hear him talk about that.

Instead, in black yoga pants that hugged her curves like he wanted to and a scrunchy, white long-sleeved top, she curled her toes into the carpet and put her hands on her hips.

Red. Her toenails were brilliant red, a flag in front of a bull, and it was the only "unprofessional" part about her. Her hair was still pulled back in the severe braid, and he wondered how the strands would look released. Hell, he wanted to know how *Kalinda* would look released, unchained from her need to control and run everything.

If he asked her, she'd probably give him a one-finger salute or tell him to take a flying leap. Maybe if he got her *really* relaxed, she'd do it for him. He wanted to grip those strands.

Wait … no. That was odd. He wanted her, sure, but it was never to the point of complete distraction. She was talking, and he refocused on her.

"Can you be serious for just one minute?" She raised a brow. "I get it. You're the consummate jokester and don't take life seriously, but *I* take mine seriously, and I want answers to my questions."

"You misunderstand my joking," he protested.

"Oh? How so?"

"I take you very seriously, Kalinda. I take any threat to your life as a threat to mine. Don't think I don't take everything about you seriously."

"What's my mother's name?"

That caught him off guard. "What?"

She smiled pretty she-wolf style, full of sharp canines, if she'd had them. That was *hot*. Her lips were full and plump. He could imagine them in places, and that image was enough to nearly bring him to his knees. It was real, her naked, dark nipples hard, her slim waist flaring into rounded hips, and her legs open to show her pretty—

Dammit.

What was wrong with him? It was like he could see the vision superimposing on the world around him. He could smell desire in the air, both his and Kalinda's, but he could scent her agitation too. The agitation brought his attention back.

"I asked you what my mother's name was."

He narrowed his eyes. Whenever he tried to have a serious conversation with her, she batted him away and walked off. That could be his fault because he usually started out by going into his default mode: heavy-handed flirting. Hell, it worked with literally every other woman he'd ever met, but not Kalinda. "I don't know."

"What is my favorite color?"

"Red?"

She looked down at her toes. "Nice try, but no. Okay, what do I like to eat?"

Romano got the point she was making, but it didn't mean he had to like it or understand why she was making it. "I don't know that either. What does that matter?"

She frowned at him and shook her head. "Let's leave this conversation at 'you are here to protect me and do a job.' Don't make it about me."

"But it is about you. Just because I don't know the answers I haven't been given the chance to learn doesn't mean I don't take you seriously."

She hmphed and strolled to the kitchen. Damn, but he liked the way she moved. His gaze was locked on to her ass when, feeling like a horny teenager, he was lost once more in the vision. The scent of old power—ash and deep earth—tinged into the room. He pulled back, looking around. Where was it coming from? It didn't make sense. None of his alarms were going off, and no one would be stupid enough to come directly to pack lands.

Romano kept one eye on Kalinda as she opened cabinets and shook her head every time she found more of her things. He kept watching for any danger coming their way as she began to cook. In a few minutes, his place smelled good enough to make his mouth water. The smell of old power was gone.

"What are you going to make?"

She startled, as if she'd forgotten he was there. "A potato and sausage soup."

He followed his nose to the kitchen, sniffing and picking up garlic and herbs cooking in the pot with pieces of bacon. He was happy her fridge was fully stocked and had brought over her supplies as well. She'd had her home filled better than most restaurants, and he wasn't sure how long she'd have to remain on the compound.

"What made you start cooking?"

She shrugged. "It calms me down."

He frowned, and she laughed—small sound that was captured nearly as quickly as it began. He liked the sound of it and would have to make her do it again.

"I don't know how to explain it. I always liked being in the kitchen and making good food. To watch how people felt when they took a bite and it soothed their soul. Something about a good, homecooked meal makes people relax. My mother always worked several jobs to help pay for things as we grew up."

"We?"

Her face darkened. "My sister and I. Mom paid for everything and made sure we didn't work. Not even in college. Cooking for Mom started out as a way to help out around the house, but eventually, I realized I loved it and decided to go to school for it."

He decided to shelve asking questions about her sister or mother. He'd heard from Zoey she'd lost her mother a few years before. The wound of it was still raw. Messing with her was much different than hurting her. He wouldn't do that.

"Did they see if you were a hearth witch?"

She shook her head. "When they scanned me for registration, the only thing that came up was my ability to moderately induce comfort through my cooking. They weren't even sure how I did that either, but it was enough for me to be remanded to an Enchanted Zone."

Romano couldn't relate to having not grown up among others like him. He was a Born Wolf and had never lived in regular society, but he'd heard horror stories of those who'd been taken from their life and families just to come to places like Encantado.

Non-magics were terrified of people with magic abilities, even if their magic was so mild it barely existed. They were frightened of its power, so they shuffled off those who made them feel threatened into cities located near the inter-dimensional portals which had torn open decades ago, spilling magic into the world.

Most people who lived in the portal areas had some level of magic. But in the general population across the United States, there were also random mutations of people who had developed magical abilities ever since the 1950s.

The moment they were discovered, they were relocated to a portal city. Sometimes their families went with them, sometimes they didn't.

"I'm sorry," he murmured. "You've fared better than a lot of people, but I'm sure it's still been hard on you, leaving everything behind."

"Sometimes." She shrugged, trying for casual, but he could hear the undercurrent of pain in her voice.

It was probably the first real conversation he'd had with her, a glimpse into another side, and he could see, maybe, why she thought he was only playing with her. He'd been in her life for months because of Zoey but had never really talked to her this way. So much for Dominic coming to him for advice on women. It seemed Romano needed to get some himself.

He watched Kalinda silently for a few more minutes. When the earthy smell returned, he surreptitiously left her to investigate but still found nothing. Stalking to his guest room, he checked in there last. He'd put most of her clothing and items into that room for her. He'd known she wouldn't have liked sharing his room, even if he'd have preferred that. His first priority, still, was to understand why someone wanted to hurt her and what that would mean.

For all intents and purposes, Kalinda was simply a business owner in District 17 without any connections to large sums of money or powerful friends. Even with knowing Zoey, it didn't make her a part of the pack, and she wouldn't be privy to insider knowledge. Anyone in Encantado would understand that but be leery of messing with her just the same. The fact they'd targeted her anyway was a problem.

A big one.

He grabbed his spell phone and dialed Dominic, who picked up after a couple of rings. "Was there anything at her home?"

"Nothing. It's clean, and the only scents were hers and what seems to be the mailman's. Nothing was out of place, nothing searched through, and all of her documentation matches what she told us. Kalinda Thorton is a Level-2 mage who owns Kalinda's Katering."

Dominic sighed. "I was really hoping not to call Zahara."

"Something personal there?"

"You don't remember, do you? I wondered why you didn't react to me saying something about her."

"Remember what?"

"How you healed."

Romano didn't remember much about the time, years ago, when he was thrown through a portal into the Chaos Realm and Dominic pulled him back out. The trolls that had shown up during their monthly warrior-class guard service hadn't been expected, neither had the portal. One minute he was fighting for his life with Dominic, and the next he was being dragged into darkness where he'd felt literally pulled apart and brought back together in so many pieces, and not all of them were his. But no, he didn't remember much of it, except in dreams, and he didn't recall them when he woke up.

"Romano?"

"Yep. Crying about the Chaos Realm over here. Thanks for the recollection."

"You're a bastard, but I like that about you. That's about all I like," Dominic mused. "Where was I? Anyway, Zahara was brought in to help heal us. Yeah, shifters heal fast, but troll wounds and portal energy are something else entirely."

"Why would she bother me though?"

"Because your wolf thought she was an enemy and tried to kill her a few times. She's going to charge us out the ass the minute you come in."

"I'll cover what it takes. If my wolf was agitated, it saw her as an enemy. I didn't try to go back and tear her to pieces, so she should have sent me a thank you note," Romano smirked.

"Yeah, don't push your luck." Romano heard the annoyance in his *Capo's* voice, and it made him smile even wider. "The Viscount Pride's involvement bothers me though. The allergy was a ruse; we know that."

Of course, it was. No shifter would eat something they were allergic to unless it was the first time and they didn't know. "But why did they need the ruse?"

"They're working for someone else?"

"Maybe, but we won't know for sure without more investigation. I'll give Zahara a call and see if she's willing to make a house visit. Until then, keep Kalinda preoccupied while we sniff out her business."

"Got it. Let me know if you find anything. She'll start asking questions soon enough."

Dominic was off the call without saying anything else.

I guess I'll get some grub then.

The soup was sizzling as he came back into the kitchen and Kalinda was mixing something else. Her hands moved faster than he'd ever seen a simple human's go, and his hackles rose.

"What are you doing now?"

When she looked at him, everything froze. Her pupils were dilated, her mouth parted on a pant. *What the hell?* Old and new, desire and need, desperation and fear all permeated the room, and now he had a direction—Kalinda.

"Food," was her only response.

Her voice wrapped around his manhood and wouldn't let go. He'd never in his life heard a woman sound like that with the most mundane word. It shouldn't have made him hard as a rock, but it did. He took a step forward, his wolf pushing and snapping.

"Kalinda?"

She blinked and picked up her spoon before bringing it to her mouth. Her pink tongue darted out and lapped at the chocolate mix she'd been working on.

Before he could stop himself, Romano took another step, and another, until he was within reaching distance. "What are you doing?"

"Eating."

She was totally hinting about something else, something I'd be more than happy to take her up on, right here in this room.

Her eyes traveled down his body, stopping between his legs before she lapped at the chocolate again. He swore her warm, wet tongue slicked its way over the head of his shaft. He slammed his hands to the table, trying to snap her out of it. As much as he'd like to take her on the island in front of her, this didn't feel right.

"Are you seeing colors, Kalinda?"

"Mocha and olive. And maybe pink, if you'd like."

That would be her, him, and … *fuck.*

Nope, he was not doing this. He gripped his spell phone like a talisman and redialed his last call.

"Romano, I swear to fuck you have the worst damn timin—"

"Yeah, so I think hot stuff here is giving me a virtual blowjob."

"You called me about *that?*"

"She's not controlling it."

Rustling on the other side of the line sounded loud in his ears. Tongues licked their way down his shaft and over his balls, and he groaned. *Not. Going. To. Make. It.*

"Romano? If you touch one hair on her head and she's not willing, I'll take your balls."

"Hello, Zoey-who's-not-sweet-anymore, she's trying to seduce me, and I'm *calling* you. I think I deserve some brownie points."

A mouth, hot like lava, wrapped around his balls, all while Kalinda stood to the side and sucked on the spoon of mix.

"Is her magic spilling again?"

Zoey's voice helped put a leash on his libido long enough for him to take a whiff. Old magic, ancient even, wafted into his nostrils.

"Tell Dominic to get Zahara here. *Now.*"

"What's happening to Kalinda?"

"Now, Zoey!"

He didn't mean to yell, he really didn't, especially when his Alpha got on the phone and the power still reached him, though it was nowhere near as strong as if he were beside him.

"You yell at my mate again and I'll end you."

"Kalinda needs help," Romano coughed out.

Sexy and skillful as she was, Romano would not allow Kalinda to be used when she wasn't aware of what she was doing. *When* they came together, she'd know exactly what she was dealing with and love every minute of it.

"Stand by."

Dominic was gone, and Romano kept the island between him and Kalinda. She sucked harder on the spoon, and he clenched the granite until it cracked under the pressure. Her tongue swirled, and his wolf whimpered in need and agony. When she used the flat of her tongue to travel from the base of the spoon near her hand and all the way back to the tip, he pulverized the rock between them and lunged for her.

Heat radiated from her hot enough to rival the sun, and she rocked her hips into his. Hard and in pain, he ignored it and cupped her face in his palms.

"Kalinda, come back to me, baby. I know you're there and this isn't what you want. Not like this. I swear to fuck I won't let you be taken this way. Ever. Listen to me. Follow my words back."

She blinked, her pupils growing wider until they swallowed her eyes in darkness. He fell into that gaze—spiraling stars and exploding universes—and he remembered it.

The Chaos Realm.

CHAPTER *Four*

old, spiked ground wanted to eat Kalinda alive, and not in the good way. Her pulse jumped and moved, from her neck, to her hands, and even to her feet. Where was her heart? It was there somewhere, wasn't it? Oh, there it went, jumping through the darkness, a little white rabbit rushing against time.

No, that wasn't right.

Hmm.

Where was she?

Oh, yum. Romano. He was hot, his heat drawing her until she couldn't think or breathe. The air here was thick. She'd always heard the phrase "thick enough to cut" but she'd never felt it until now. It started angry, raging even, burning against her flesh and sizzling away cells and slipping into the missing pieces. The locks broke within her, spinning and turning, tumblers sliding into place, and those black, ugly spots changed. They set on fire, flaring brighter than the sun, eclipsing the darkness until she wanted nothing but skin.

Romano's skin.

Close.

She wanted to feel him, taste him. Where was he? She couldn't find him, and it pissed her off. She needed him, and the asshole always threatened to eat her alive. Well, now she wanted to eat *him*.

Something was wrong. Her mind kept splintering, fracturing and running away. Tumbling chaotically through thoughts, holding on to them like sands slipping through her fingers.

Fingers, oh, around Romano's shaft, pumping him until he was stiff and hard, his soft skin slick with his need and her saliva. That's what she wanted. It all made sense now. She searched for that, pulling to get him closer, to find his heat, his desire. She craved him and was finished denying herself.

But would there be a tomorrow?

Come this way, little mage. Hungry mage. We can feed you.

What?

Finally looking around her, she realized she was in a place she'd never seen before. Jagged shards of obsidian grass pierced a swampy black ground. The earth twisted and moved like oil and water wrapping around her ankles.

Come, come, mage. We will make you stronger.

No. She didn't want to be stronger. She wanted to get out.

"Please, help me!"

Her voice went out and came back, slapping her in the face with the force of torrential wind before slipping her off her feet.

Welcome home.

She screamed again, but there was no sound. Her wail was only a raw bite in her throat. Terror clogged her chest, making it hard to breathe with each gasp, pulling at her hair, yanking on her skin, ripping into her and twisting her up.

Although she was afraid and her mind fought against each step with fright to freeze her, somehow, she recognized this feeling. In her blood, the metals of her existence sang. They rejoiced to be back here. To touch chaos once again.

Chaos.

Something about that made sense, but it was too late and it slipped away. She couldn't hold on to anything more than desire for Romano or the feeling of homecoming into the sharp, inky night. Which one was real? Or was any of it? She couldn't make sense of it.

"She's deep in there. Let me look at the child."

The woman's voice wrapped around her, anchoring her. The accent was thick, but Kalinda couldn't place it. The one thing she did know was when she heard it, her mind cleared.

"I'm here. Right here."

"I have you. Feel me now?"

Her voice was a rope, rough-hewn twine, wrapped around Kalinda's ankle and tethering her to the ground, wherever that was.

"Now hold on, gal, while I work."

There wasn't much else Kalinda could do. For now, she peered around, floating in the air, the oppressing feeling of the air. Now she saw everything wasn't black but *shades* of black. The grass and ground were the darkest, like an abstract painting of splattered monochrome. The space in between the—sky?—was more gray and murky, a thick fog coiled and ready to strike. Kalinda floated above it all in a navy-blue, starless sky.

Not exactly.

As she watched, small flames of gray and almost white hovered just before her. She couldn't look away if she wanted to.

"Hello, daughter. We see you. We will forever see you now. When you go home, we shall follow."

Um, no. I'd rather you didn't.

A wry, warped chuckle filled the air. "You don't have a choice. You need us now."

"You can hear me?"

"Quiet, I'm working." *That* was not the flames but the one who anchored her.

"Yes, we hear you. In here, speak in your mind, as you did before. The others won't understand."

Like this?

"Well met, young one. You will need us in the time to come. Do not fear the darkness. It was meant to be at your fingertips."

I never asked for any of this.

"Neither did we. Neither did we."

The rope jerked and the flames shot at her, slamming into her heart and making her scream before she was pulled harder.

"You belong in this world, love. Come home."

Another yank, and Kalinda was spiraling, splintering, and put back together. She couldn't tell which was up or down, but she smashed apart before jerking out into the sun.

"Jesus, Kalinda."

She blinked. It took a moment, but she was able to recognize Romano's guest room. He leaned over her, worried eyes scanning her.

"I'm okay," she croaked. Not that she was sure, but she refused to be weak. She tried to sit up as another face swam into view.

"Rihanna?"

Freaking Rihanna was there, with some amazing white lines down the bridge of her nose and dots under her eyes. Her top lip was white as well, and her wild, dark hair was kinky around her shoulders. She smiled, showing pearly white teeth.

"I've heard that a lot. Must be the blood of the islands in us all. I'm Zahara. And you, pretty girl, are extraordinary." She leaned forward suddenly, her eyes going dark as night. "The flames burn hot in you. Will you catch fire, or play?"

"How about run? I like that answer."

Zahara blinked, and her face cleared. "We shall see, won't we?" She looked at Romano, her lip curling. "I'm charging extra for dog bites. You know that, right?"

Romano rolled his shoulders, worry lining his face, but his smile was razor sharp. "Only if you survive them."

Zahara looked him up and down. "Looks like you got your snap back, even if you tried to take a bite out of my ass. I still want to put you into a dark place for a very long time for that."

"I can't be blamed for my wolf wanting to protect me."

"Don't be so sure." Zahara flicked her hands up in the air in his direction before she frowned down at Kalinda. "She's out of the woods for now."

"But what happened?"

This time Zoey came into view, rubbing her belly and tears filling her eyes. Kalinda didn't remember seeing Zoey cry, ever, and it nearly scared her as much as being in the dark place.

"I'm okay, Zoey. Really."

"You didn't see it, Kalinda."

"But I'm here now."

Zoey managed a smile that looked more like a grimace. "Look at you … taking care of me when you're the one who should have everyone caring for her."

Kalinda shrugged. She'd never been comfortable with people caring for her like that. People didn't … stay. "Damn, I feel like I've been hit by a dump truck."

"You look it too," Zoey quipped.

"Oh, thanks, that makes me feel grand."

"Don't listen to her," Romano said. "I'd eat you and go back for seconds, I'm just saying."

Kalinda rolled her eyes at the last statement. Of course, *he'd* say that. Instead of focusing on how it felt to have them around—or how good it felt to have him there for her—she looked to Zahara again.

What mattered was what had happened to her. "Where was I?"

Before she could answer, Romano huffed. "Zoey, you're doing that miracle grow thing again." Kalinda had no idea what the hell he was talking about, but his eyes were glued to a potted orchid in the corner of the room. It was … massive—larger than any orchid she'd ever seen—and little gold dust floated around it.

"Did you just call my mate *fertilizer*?" Dominic forced out. Kalinda couldn't tell if he wanted to laugh, growl, or a mixture of both.

Romano whirled on him. "Well, what else am I supposed to call it? Magic poopourri or something?"

"I'm going to punch you."

"I'm just saying, D."

"Still going to punch you."

"Sorry," Zoey quipped, and she stepped back a bit, away from Romano.

What. The. Hell? The damn orchid shrank back to normal size, but the petals were a bit wilted.

Kalinda pointed to the plant. "Um, what was that?"

Zoey shrugged. "We don't know, honestly. But it's not important right now. Zahara? What happened to Kalinda?"

Okay, I'll file that for later 'cause, you know, sudden plant explosion isn't weird at all.

"She was in the Chaos Realm, of course," Zahara stated it like it was child's play.

Everyone sucked in a breath and then started talking at once.

"What?"

"How?"

"Is she safe?"

The last was from Romano. Smart. It seemed

Zahara lifted her hands, quieting the room. "She pulled her magic from there and got lost in it. That's how. As for why she got lost, it's because she's been a very naughty girl and hasn't been practicing with it."

"Wait, stop. I have no idea what you're talking about. I've never been able to use magic like that. The most I can do is put good vibes in food."

Kalinda was really tired of explaining this. It irritated her how much things had changed lately, but she hadn't caused any of it. It was like getting mixed up with shifters and their shenanigans had turned the whole world upside down.

She didn't hate them—that would be silly and unfair—but she didn't like things she couldn't control. Her catering company ran smoothly, and she went home every night to dream up new business opportunities and leave it at that. She didn't have to deal with the stress of a relationship, family depending on her, or finding a way to save herself from sliding into some godforsaken realm where flames spoke to her!

Over it.

She wanted to go back home, curl under her cover, and realize this was all a damn dream. A bad one, but a dream all the same. She sat up to do just that. Forget *all* of this.

"The Council of Mages will come for you soon."

Zahara was officially queen of shutting down a room instantly. No one moved for an entire minute, including Kalinda.

"Why?" she finally forced out, looking at the witch doctor.

"Because you will be one of them ... if you accept. You can become powerful enough to be one. If they find out, they will come for you."

"I don't understand. I'm Level 2. They have already swept me."

"Things change. The old magic is in you. I can't tell you more than that, and I don't care for them anyway, so I won't share your secret. You can't hide this forever though."

Romano stepped forward. "Can you tell what her magic is changing to? I've smelled something ancient on her, and it's even stronger now." At Kalinda's dirty look, he added, "Ancient and *delicious.*"

Yeah, that helped. Not.

Romano moved and sat on the bed, wrapping his arms around her. Kalinda let him hold her, soaking in his strength for a few moments and acting like she had someone to lean on again—someone she could trust. She hadn't realized how much she'd missed it. How much it soothed her. He didn't disappoint. Rubbing his hands up and down her spine, a soft growl that was oddly soothing rumbled his chest.

Zahara shrugged. "I don't know, but I would wager she is closer to me now."

"What does that mean?"

Kalinda appreciated Romano taking the lead in questioning. She knew she was wide-eyed, but she couldn't help it. It was all too hard to take in.

"A Level 9, if she can control it. It hasn't manifested all the way, so it fluctuates. I can't read past that, or her form. It's still shrouded. I'll take payment in my account before I've left the grounds. If I don't receive, your pack lands will be gone."

Dominic growled but wisely stayed silent and nodded as Zahara left. In the mage caste system, the ten levels didn't mean a small step up. Each level jumped exponentially, depending on the skillset.

For example, a Level 1 one may have just a twinge of magic, enough to be caught in a sweep. The next level would have more of a spark and be able to manifest said magic in small ways. Like Zoey with her map magic which let her find her way anywhere and her ability to make flowers bloom, or Kalinda with her adding comfort to her food.

From there, the levels of power jumped up in larger manifestations. Levels 8 through 10 are Council levels, and a Level 9 would be able to challenge the power of an Alpha for a time. There was no way Kalinda would believe she was the same level as Dominic. None of this made sense, and she was *sick* of not understanding.

She had no interest in being tied up with the Council or the FBMC. They'd ruined her life to begin with, and she was not in the mood.

She wrenched out of Romano's arms and stood on shaky feet. She felt bruised everywhere, but nothing was going to stop her from going home and leaving all of this behind.

"Where are you going?"

She ignored Romano. Instead, she stomped her way past a smirking Zoey.

"Ohhhh. Someone's in trouble."

Kalinda stopped herself, barely, from growling. "Can it, Sunshine. I'm done with it."

"Can't can it," Zoey smirked. "I tried, and they told me I was too addicting. Besides, Dominic would just buy every can off the shelf and threaten to rip off the arms of anyone who thought to buy it."

"Go have your baby already," Kalinda retorted.

"Hey, friends don't wish pain on friends."

"I'm wishing a bundle of joy and lots of extra time lost here so you can't bother me. Big difference, chick. Big difference."

She didn't know how she was going to get all her things home but she was *going*. She tucked her feet into her Chucks—the only time she didn't wear heels was when she was home—and looked for her purse.

Zahara, the purveyor of the crazy times, simply walked out the door without a care while Zoey, Dominic, and Romano followed the tornado called Kalinda as she stormed through the house to pick up what she could carry.

"I'm going to ask again because I'm starting to worry that maybe your hearing isn't working." Romano stopped in front of her, his massive form blocking her from leaving the kitchen. Okay, the stuff in her arms was *really* heavy, and she was not in the mood.

Countdown to complete meltdown, starting now.

"Where are you going?" Romano quirked a brow.

"Home. Where else? I'm not some great mage who deserves to be on the Council."

"Zahara doesn't get things wrong. If she says that's the power you're coming into, then it is."

Not listening.

Okay, so she may be a little childish right now. Okay, a lot. But she was terrified of what this would mean, and she didn't understand any of it. Not the flames. Not the Chaos Realm or how she could get there, none of it. And not understanding made her very nervous. Feeling nervous pissed her off. Kalinda needed space, her own four walls, and some way to get this all off her mind.

She needed to bake thirty cakes and maybe a thousand cookies. Whatever.

Romano moved with her when she tried to go around him. "For now, you *are* home. Go have some rest and then we can think about what Zahara has told us. If she needs to come again, we can get her out here."

T-minus ten seconds and counting.

"Get out of my way and let me go."

"Can't. Been told I have glue on my hands. Sort of makes things stick. Want me to show you how fun that can be?"

T-minus nine seconds.

"We're going to head out. Call if you need anything." Zoey had the nerve to wave her fingers over her shoulder before Dominic ushered her out. The woman wanted to die.

T-minus eight seconds.

"Maybe we can enjoy the soup you made. Are you hungry?"

"No, I'm not. I want a big, hulking brute to get out of my way."

"Oh, big *and* hulking. You say the sweetest things and I haven't even shown you the biggest part yet."

He wants to die. I know it. T-minus seven seconds. Six, five, four …

She jerked her knee up, fed up and wanting to get out desperately. Her chest tightened and a knot formed in her throat. She was losing it, twisting and turning down fear. Control. She needed it. Had to have it. Without it, things got lost.

"Not happening, sweetheart."

"I am *not* your sweetheart."

Three, two, one …

One minute, her arms were laden with her items, and the next, everything crashed to the floor. She didn't understand it, but she was flying off the handle, leaping at Romano in a fit to get out and be free. The door was so close and yet so far.

"Easy there. I got you. You're going to hurt yourself."

It didn't matter. She wanted *out*. To escape, to compartmentalize so she could regain some semblance of who she was. She panted, trying to suck in deeper breaths, but it was like using a coffee straw.

"Come here."

Romano took her into his arms again, carrying her away from the carnage in his living room and past the guest room. In a few more steps, he kicked open a door to a large, darkened room. She caught a glimpse of deep mahogany and crimson that blurred together moments before she flopped down on a bed.

The door slammed shut, closing them in, and she scrambled back on the bed away from him. He didn't let her go far, gripping her ankle and yanking her down to the end of the bed. It was just like in the Chaos Realm, when Zahara had given her something to hold on to, and she couldn't help the sense of calm that came over her, a momentary peace.

"Tell me what you need. What I saw a moment ago was panic, and I understand panic," he whispered.

His voice was so much more because he didn't speak loudly. He hovered over her, his weight just inches away, his mouth closing in on hers.

"Tell me what you *really* need and I'll give it to you. But leaving when you know it isn't safe isn't a decision the Kalinda I know would make."

Romano's lips danced over hers with each word—a taunt, a promise. She found herself mesmerized, her breathing slowing to match his. He never looked away from her. It was one of the most intimate moments she'd ever had without a single stich of clothing being gone. He saw *her* and asked her what she needed.

Kalinda swallowed, afraid to speak but unable to stop herself. "I don't know."

His large hand, warm and familiar, cupped her chin, his thumb caressing her bottom lip. "You don't always have to have the answer. It's okay to be lost."

She couldn't respond. Not when his mouth claimed hers. Not when he set her ablaze with silken lips and a skillful tongue that traced the seam of her closed mouth and demanded entrance. She let him in on a sigh, and he devoured her.

Nothing with him came easily. He filled her, tasting every crevice of her mouth, laying claim in a way she hadn't thought possible. The only place they were connected were by their mouths and his hand on her chin, but she felt his weight pressing in on her. He may as well have fully rested his weight down on her.

She let him lead, following his tongue and letting go. Her nipples hardened in her bra, and she felt achy in a new way. She was tempted to curl her fingers into his shirt, to rip it from his body and take what she knew he would offer, but she knew she'd regret it. That she'd hate that she was so weak. The longer he kissed her, though, the more that thought faded until she was all molten heat and need. Kalinda trembled with it and needed more.

When their lips parted, she was willing to say yes to his next question.

"Get some rest, Kalinda. I'll be here to watch over you. I promise."

Instead, Romano gave her what she needed when she hadn't even known it herself. Security.

CHAPTER *FIVE*

Okay, so she was woman enough to admit she was running. Three days of being cooped up in the house with the ever-present panty annihilator who touched her all the time but never went beyond that—which she didn't want, of course … *right*—had stretched her nerves thin. She needed to run, to get some fresh air, and return to her business. She knew the Viscount Pride probably still had beef with her, but after three days, no summons from them or the Council had come forth. Zahara may have never been wrong before, but there was always a first time. Kalinda hadn't had any flare-ups since that first day either.

Zoey had spilled the beans, to the complete embarrassment of Kalinda, that she'd somehow magicked a blowjob but hadn't exactly finished the job when Romano called for help. How was she to know what was brewing between them was real and not the magic she'd used? Sure, she'd been attracted to him before the flare-ups got bad, but she'd only met him around the time her magic started changing, and it seemed she unconsciously used the power.

For now, there was too much to think about and too much time to think about it. She'd had to allow Silva to run the business the last few days, and thank God she had the Fae, but that didn't mean Kalinda could afford to be away from her business indefinitely. Silva told her orders were coming in from The Daily Grind, and

Kalinda had to keep up with that engagement. It was too important.

So Kalinda had a plan: find Lorenzo and see if he could help get her out of there.

Lorenzo was a low-level fire mage teenager who'd been taken under the protection of the pack. He also had a super protective mother, and as a result, he'd developed mad skills at sneaking, evading, and escaping supervision when he wanted to.

Romano had been called to handle something in the main house, and it gave Kalinda enough time to make her move. It was now or never. She'd put on jogging clothes and her tennis shoes and tucked her phone and keys into her bra. Not the most comfortable, but it kept her hands free and looked a lot less like she was planning an escape. She took a lap around the edge of the compound. It was much larger than she'd expected. The pack lands were comprised of a subdivision with Dominic's home and his Enforcers living around his location. After working up a pretty good sweat, she figured she'd been seen by enough wolves to disappear.

After a short distance, she veered off her path in search of one of the teens Dominic's pack had taken in and built a community center for. When they weren't in the apartments he'd had built for them, they spent a lot of their time working on pack lands and had gained a sense of family. Cin's jewelry was highly sought after around town, and if she kept going the way she was, her growth would be very good for her nationally too.

Lorenzo would be ideal. His best friend Heath would do in a pinch. Years of living on the street had made him good at dodging just about anyone: cops, store owners he'd just boosted merchandise from, or security guards. And sure, Lorenzo, Cin, and Heath were grateful to the wolves for helping them out, but they were still kids. And they still loved the chance make a little mischief sometimes.

She spotted Cin and Lorenzo a few hundred feet away, standing in a clearing sharing the headphones from Lorenzo's spell phone. Heath sat on the ground with his knees drawn up under his chin and watched them with an odd expression on his face. Kalinda felt bad for him. He was kind of a third wheel these days.

Well, maybe helping her escape would take his mind off things for a minute. She started to head their way.

"Out for a stroll?"

Kalinda nearly tripped and fell flat on her face when Giuliana paced next to her, barely breathing hard. The wolf, she was sure, could run for miles without tiring. The benefit of her genetics.

"Yes, for now."

Giuliana's brow arched at that. "Oh? Do tell."

"Depends. Are you still a master of escaping?"

She wasn't Lorenzo, but Giuliana had dealt with her oppressive uncle, Arturo, tracking her wherever she went and keeping her from having much of a life. Now that she had joined Dominic's pack, she had a lot more freedom. She'd been able to open a vintage clothing shop, and she no longer had her uncle tracking her movements every moment of every day. She was still pack, however, and Kalinda couldn't be sure she would help, wild streak or not.

Giuliana shrugged. "Depends on who you're running from."

Kalinda bit her lip. She wasn't exactly sure she was ready for that conversation. *Yet.*

"Ah, Romano." Giuliana nodded in understanding. "He's not a bad guy, not really. His parents messed him up pretty badly, you know?"

Kalinda hadn't heard about that. All she'd ever gotten from him were jokes and double entendre. Oh, and hot-as-fuck need pouring off of him. But the parents thing intrigued her. "How?"

"Ask him sometime. As to escaping, I suppose I could help, for a couple hours at least. But if my Alpha asks, I'll tell him where you are."

Well, a few hours to get her head straight was better than nothing. "Fine. I just need to go by my house and clean up before checking in at the office. I may need to make some orders, and there are plenty of baked goods in there for you as payment."

"Done. Let's head to my car."

That was easy.

Ten minutes later, they were passing through the exterior guard post out of Lombardi Pack lands and into the city proper. Another fifteen minutes and she was nearly to her home. Kalinda damn near felt like she could cry.

Giuliana leaned over and inhaled deeply. "You smell different."

"I'm really tired of hearing that. You know, that will give a girl a complex."

"It isn't unpleasant, but you normally smell like chocolate or vanilla, you know, food. Now it's food *and* old magic. It's wild."

"Had a run-in with the Chaos Realm," Kalinda hedged. She wasn't sure how much Romano or Dominic had shared, but she wouldn't give away more information than she needed to.

Giuliana cut her gaze at Kalinda but didn't ask anything else. Probably respected the boundary since she'd put one up herself about Romano. Once in her home, Kalinda took a much-needed shower, changed into her work gear, complete with her favorite heels, and headed back out.

"Ready?"

"As ready as I'll ever be. Doesn't seem like I'll have enough time to hang out and relax in my own home."

Giuliana winced. "I know it doesn't help, but if Dominic wants you protected, he has a reason. He really isn't one to overreact, and trust me, I know all about that."

Yeah, she did, and Kalinda wouldn't argue with that. Still, it chaffed not being able to be her own person anymore. It seemed like it was all an overreaction for no reason.

Heading into her office was uneventful as well. When they got there, Silva was moving around outside in front of cargo vans loading platters and giving work details as if she'd been doing it for years.

"Tatiana, you have the Baker party. Lily, get what we have over to The Daily Grind and tell Danielle or Tony that Kalinda will get the rest of their order to them as soon as possible. Jasmine, you have the Walkers, and we're good for the day. I'll head out to do some rounds and keep up with reservations."

She was a regular drill sergeant. To keep down a whole lot of questions, Kalinda waited until everyone left for their posts before she got out of the car and headed in. Silva met her at the front door.

"I thought that was you. Are you okay?"

"It's all a precaution right now, but thanks for running everything. Looks like I don't need to even be here."

Silva wrinkled her nose. "Okay, where is my boss and what have you done to her?"

Kalinda laughed, and it was the first time she'd felt free in a while. Everything that had been happening weighed heavily on her shoulders, and even for someone as serious as her, it was a lot. *But ...*

Kalinda stood up tall, wiped her hands down her front before making sure her bun was neat and secure on top of her head. "Where are we with the order from The Daily Grind?"

"There she is." Silva smiled softly. "You've got orders for twenty whole lemon cakes, a hundred assorted muffins, add in an assortment of coffee cakes and Danishes. Danielle added for you to hurry it up. She's getting cranky, like when she has no coffee."

Kalinda snorted. "She owns a coffee shop; she's never out of coffee."

"Just passing on the message."

"Heard, loud and clear. I suppose I should get to work, and Giuliana, you get meals for babysitting."

Silva looked over Giuliana quizzically. "Wolf?"

"Got it in one. Hi, I'm Giuliana, resident babysitter for the day." She extended her hand to Silva.

There was an awkward moment of silence as Silva stared at Giuliana's hand. Kalinda frowned, wondering what that was all about.

"I won't bite," Giuliana commented with a hesitant laugh.

"That's what they all say."

"Well, you could just try it out."

Silva shrugged and shook her hand but snatched it back as if burned. Giuliana did the same, eyes widening. "You're—"

"A worker for Kalinda, and it's nice to meet you. The vintage shop is yours, I think?"

"Um, yes."

Well, that wasn't weird at all.

Kalinda wondered at the interaction, but Silva turned to lead them into the shop before she could ask any questions. Still, Kalinda wasn't going to let it go, and would have to get Silva alone to understand what had happened.

Silva had been an odd hire for Kalinda after losing Zoey. She'd had experience in baking, managing, and customer service skills to boot, making her an instant attractive prospect. But she'd had no references, no real history, and didn't seem like she wanted to share it much. Living in portal cities wasn't exactly the safest place to be, and Kalinda had gotten used to the certain level of anonymity the people liked to have at times, but Silva still pushed the envelope into crazy-weird.

Her interview had consisted of baking a three-tier cake, each layer made from a different flavor, then assisting with serving while managing clients. She'd excelled at it all, impressing Kalinda greatly. But in the time she'd known Silva, Kalinda hadn't found out much of her past except she was Fae and had no intention of living within Fae land borders.

The inside of the shop smelled of flour, sweets, and food, a scent that soothed Kalinda instantly. *This* she knew and understood. Her kitchen gleamed from the polished stainless steel, thanks to Silva who, it seemed, had stayed diligent in keeping it that way.

"Giuliana, I'll be in here for some time working. If you'd like, you can be in my seating area. I have cable and a setup in there for you to be comfortable."

"Sweet! I can catch some DIY shows while I'm at it."

The wolf was gone instantly, and Silva released a breath.

"Silva, you're on sous."

For a time, they worked silently, Kalinda pushing her magic into food as she chopped, blended, and slid batter into the oven. She had cuts of prime rib warming for Giuliana and figured enough time had passed she could ask what was going on with Silva.

"What was that earlier?"

Silva's hands froze for a moment before she went back to mixing her frosting for the coffee cakes. "I don't know what you mean."

Kalinda lifted a brow. "You know me better than that by now."

"It's not something I like talking about. Where have you been?"

"Is this one of those 'I'll show you mine and you show me yours' moments?"

"Maybe."

Silva never looked up, but Kalinda could sense this was important. She sighed. "The whole thing with the Viscount Pride seems to lead the wolves to believe the lions are attracted to my changing magic."

"It has been arcing lately."

"Jeez, it seems everyone but me noticed it."

"You noticed. You just didn't think about what it could mean. You're a workaholic, Kalinda, and everyone knows that. I was surprised you could stay away from this place for a few days, despite what happened."

"It's my business."

"And your shield."

Kalinda looked up and met Silva's gaze. She'd never really looked into Silva's eyes before, and now could see they were green with a rim of purple around them. They were beautiful, but as Kalinda stared, those eyes glittered golden and the pupils dilated.

"Well … yes," Kalinda forced out. "It has become a place of comfort. I built this with my own two hands. I use my mother's old recipes every day to pay homage to all she did for me and my sister."

"And now your magic is shifting, changing, and that group, the lions, were affected by it."

Kalinda nodded. "Dominic and Romano had me checked out with Zahara." Again, she found herself skirting the truth, not sure how much of it should could share with anyone.

"Hmmm," Silva said as she packed the frosting into pastry bags for decorating later.

"Oh no, that's not the end of this. It's your turn, Tinker."

Her trademark action showed up when Silva wrinkled her nose. "I would like to tell you she was *not* Fae but a *fairy*. Much different. A sprite, or what have you, from the element of wind who could help people fly with her fairy dust. A fairy answers to the power of the Fae if it is so ordered or they are bound. I am *not* a fairy, and much cuter."

"Oh, well excuse me."

"You're excused."

"Spill."

Silva sighed and mumbled something Kalinda had no chance of hearing.

"What was that?"

"I don't know what to tell you or what I *can* tell you."

Okay, so that wasn't ominous at all … *not!* Kalinda was already pretty tired of not understanding, and she figured the last three days had proven that while her magic was changing, the danger they all thought she was in was not as immediate as they originally thought. The Viscount Pride nor the Council had made no contact, and Kalinda was starting to think there was some conspiracy going on around her, and she didn't like it.

"Not really an answer after I was truthful with you, and I won't accept it," Kalinda admonished.

"And you and I both know you didn't tell me everything, and that happens. We're both protecting something."

"How would you know if I was hiding something?"

Silva rolled her eyes. "Probably because your magic now feels older than mine, and mine is *old*, like three-wise-men, baby-in-a-manger, immaculate-conception old. No, I'm wrong, probably closer to when humans first walked the earth. But you get it. *Old*."

"Did you just say …" Yep, that was about the time Kalinda lost it. Tears rolling down her cheeks, she laughed until her sides hurt. "Wait, what sort of magic is immaculate-conception old? Who says that?"

Silva twirled her fingers before her face, laughing. "Me?"

"What does that all even mean?"

"It means your magic hasn't just changed or elevated, it's …" Silva moved her hands through the air between them. "It's hard to explain. It's not just yours anymore, and the magic added to yours is very powerful."

"Well, that's the only thing I didn't tell you, but it's because I don't really understand it. Zahara said I was touched and that the Council could be contacting me, but nothing has happened. It all seems like people keep telling me what my magic is but nothing is changing in how I can use it. It only happens in random spurts."

Silva nodded. "I can't tell you much more either. I wasn't lying when I said I don't know what to tell you or how much. I know where I come from, but the secrecy around that isn't just my own to hold, so I cannot share, but as far as why I'm here, I don't know."

"Sounds like your problem may be worse than mine."

"Tell me about it."

The timer dinged and Kalinda got her cakes out to cool before putting another batch in, along with several muffin trays. What a beautiful invention double ovens were, and she had a few of them. They made work a lot easier when she had larger orders. But still, her skin felt tight, and her normal comfort when she cooked was lost. She took the prime rib to Giuliana, who barely looked up from a show about home renovation with a quiet thank you, and Kalinda still felt off.

It was stupid, but she sort of felt like reaching out to Romano, and that made her groan out loud. She didn't need anyone, especially not their comfort, or their arms around her, or their …

What are you thinking about, K? Are you serious?

But one thought led to the next, and she couldn't stop herself from thinking about Romano. His lips, the strength in his body, the hard planes pressed against her softer curves. Okay, so she could admit he was a hot piece of man, even if annoying as hell, but she couldn't afford to get tied up with him.

He'd always flirted, but he seemed to be that way no matter whom it involved, and she couldn't take him seriously. The only interaction with him after the fact was, well, tied up into her magic that apparently wanted to jump his bones.

"This can't be happening."

Kalinda shook her head, trying to clear it, and headed back into her kitchen. Thoughts of sexy time firmly under control, she continued to work on her order. So no, she wasn't thinking about Romano's mouth, or his eyes, or his body, or the way he curled around her when she came out of the Chaos Realm. And, of course, she wasn't thinking she sort of, really, maybe just a bit, but kind of a lot, enjoyed how her magic touched him in all the right—wrong!—places.

Nope, she wasn't thinking about any of that.

She and Silva worked steadily, for hours, until she was ready to box her orders. But first, she needed to taste a bit and always made a side cake from any batter to make sure it came out well. Silva, used to her manner of working, had her fork ready.

"Should we call the babysitter in here too?" Silva didn't even look up as she asked, her gaze was firmly on the molding from the lemon cake. The girl had a serious sweet tooth.

"Probably. Hey, Giuliana, there's free cake in here!"

Silently but lightning fast, Giuliana was at their side, and Kalinda swore her expression was the human form of a dog wagging its tail.

"Can I try them all?"

Kalinda smiled. "Sure. I love when people enjoy my food."

"The prime rib was amazing. You should really make that for the pack one day. They'd love you forever."

"It may be on the menu since they're taking care of me."

"I'll let Dominic know."

Fork in hand, the ladies dug in. Kalinda always added a touch of comfort and love into her food, hoping that when people ate, they'd enjoy a sense of care and release from the stresses of their lives. She'd always loved how her magical gift may not have been something huge and showy, but it still helped people just the same.

"Whoa."

Kalinda blinked and looked over at Giuliana. "What is it?"

"Um, what did you put in this?" Giuliana gestured at the small red velvet muffin tray she was currently scooping massive bites out of.

"I didn't put anything beyond my recipe, if that's what you mean."

"No," she cleared her throat, "ingredients meant to get you hot?"

"What?"

"Yeah, I wondered that too," Silva added, fork hovering over her lemon cake. Her face was flush and her eyes wide as she licked her lips. "This shouldn't be happening. It shouldn't be possible." Her hazy gaze fastened to Kalinda's. "Okay, we may have a problem with my conception of how old your magic is."

Come to think of it, Giuliana didn't look much different, her knuckles white from clenching her fork. And what the hell was Silva talking about?

"What is wrong with you guys?"

"I don't know, but it's really hot in here. Can we open some windows?"

Before Kalinda could stop Giuliana from snapping the wards, she'd already done it, muscling through the magic and throwing the bay windows in the kitchen wide open. She fanned herself, pulling at the neckline of her shirt as she sucked in big gulps of air.

Silva danced in her seat, clenching her legs before uncrossing them. She gripped the side of the table and crossed her legs again. Then. She. Moaned. The sort of moan that said, "Right there, and don't move or you'll die." Silva let her head fall and rested her forehead on the table.

Kalinda groaned. "What have I done?"

CHAPTER *Six*

Kalinda had two withering women in her kitchen who were craving doing the vertical tango after eating cakes, and she didn't know what the hell had happened or how to fix it. She raced around, grabbing ice and giving it to them to cool off, but that was an utter disaster.

Giuliana let it slide down into her shirt and damn near ruined the paint under the window when she clawed her way to the floor. And Silva? The ice somehow *slipped* and fell between her legs. Apparently, cold isn't deterred by a cotton-based material, and that made Silva's entire day.

Like, bucking and screaming yes sort of day.

"I'm never cooking again. I swear. Never."

She tasted her food again. Maybe not be the best idea, but she hadn't been affected at all by the food she'd made.

Oh. Wait.

She did have some of that chocolate batter that resulted in the magical head. All she could figure was every time she made something, someone was getting their freak on. Kalinda groaned. Her world was turning upside down. Red faced and not knowing what else to do, she picked up her phone. The jerk picked up in two rings flat.

"Kalinda? Where are you?"

"Well—"

"Are you watching a porno? Because I could have helped with that. All you needed was to ask, baby."

Kalinda breathed and counted to ten. Of course, that only gave time for Silva to do another crazy moan that made Kalinda's ears turn red.

"I can be home in five minutes. I'll run all the way there if I have to."

Ugh! Men. "It's not a porno, you fiend. And I'm not at your house. It's … well, Silva and Giuliana."

"Come again?" He sounded far too intrigued.

Okay, she had to admit that had sounded bad. "Well, I'm in the room with them at my shop, and—"

"I mean, I'm all for experimentation, but I'm more interested in pleasing you. Wait. Did you say your shop?"

"Shut up for one second! I made food and they ate it, yes, at my shop, and now they are having sex with the air."

"Please tell me you got it on camera because I'm never going to let Giuliana live this down."

"Shut up and just get here."

"I'm already on the way. I'm bringing Dominic in case she needs Alpha power to calm Giuliana. Don't know about Silva, but we'll figure it out. Until then, if you need any help, I'm your man. I'll kick the air's ass, too, for touching you."

"Do you know how you sound right now?"

"Still true. I'm on my way."

Kalinda wasn't going to admit knowing he was on his way made her feel better. For now, she tried to keep the undulating women in a contained area and away from the treats they tried to keep coming back to. While she loved anyone coming back for seconds or thirds, she didn't think this was a good time for that at all. She tossed the cakes out of her kitchen, figuring she'd be able to clean the mess up later, and was on guard duty.

That was until the people appeared, like, out of nowhere, in front of her kitchen window.

"So *you're* the one."

The first, a tall man with pure white hair tied into a messy bun atop his head, dove-gray eyes, and at least six feet tall and middle-aged, stepped over Giuliana. Maybe the better way to say was he floated over her, landing softly in the kitchen. A woman, about as tall as Kalinda, with coal-black skin, dark eyes, straight hair down to her waist, and a dark fitted dress simply stepped over the wall of the bay window and stood at the first man's side. The last male, shorter than the others, was hard to pinpoint. It was like his features morphed and swam from non-descript to beautiful and back again, even his hair color changed. He was outside one minute, and the next, inside standing next to the three with a clap of thunder.

What the fuck?

Chills raced down her spine looking at the walking Rorschach test, and her skin crawled. *No, no, no, no.* That was creepy as hell, and she was not into scary things or movies. Her chest tightened, and it was all she could to keep from running and screaming.

Kalinda stumbled back, too afraid to say a thing. Silva, who'd been jerking and twisting, reached for something on the table. Still moaning, she gazed steadily at the people in front of her. She croaked something, but Kalinda didn't understand.

She reached again, and Kalinda saw it was a knife. "R … un."

Run? Run where? But Kalinda didn't think twice. If Silva was worried enough and had fought through the fog of whatever spell Kalinda had put on her to tell her that, she wasn't going to argue. Kalinda spun on her heel, ready to get out of her kitchen and out the front door, when a clap of thunder sounded again. Wavy Man, because that was totally his name right now, was in front of her and reached for her.

"We'd like you to be our guest."

Kalinda had never heard a voice like that. Every word was a different tone and octave, punching at her eardrums and soothing at the same time. She couldn't have ignored it if she tried.

"You're scaring me," she forced out. She knew Romano and Dominic were coming. She'd be okay once they arrived and Dominic could get Giuliana back in action.

"They won't make it."

That was from the woman behind her, and Kalinda turned sideways so she could see them both.

"The men you're waiting for. Or should I say the wolves? They won't make it here in time. But you aren't under attack, my child. We are here to help protect you. We've been searching for you for days but have been unable to find you. The wards around you have been rather strong, until today."

"If I'm not in danger, why can't we just wait until they get here?"

The white-haired man stepped forward. "Let me explain it to her, Amalia."

Amalia nodded and stepped back.

"Because the *Capo di tutti Capi* and his Enforcer cannot make this choice for you, nor does their word have authority over us. It is the other way around, as you see."

"Who are you?"

"I am Lennox. This is Amalia and Yon. We are the Trinity of the Mage Council."

Kalinda knew about the Council. No magic-blood could live outside of Enchanted Zones where there were portal cities. The Federal Bureau of Magical Containment, or the FBMC, did sweeps to find those with magic in their blood, no matter how small. The FBMC worked as a liaison between the National Council and the FBI counterpart in the non-magic world. And the direct control within Enchanted Zones was a Mage Council who answered only to the National Council.

At the top of each Mage Council was the Trinity, a group of three who could be a tiebreaker for any vote and who also stood as *the* magical last word in disputes if necessary. Very few people ever saw them.

And they all stood in Kalinda's Katering with a half-blitzed wolf and a Fae trying desperately to fend off an orgasm while attempting to stab one of the Trinity.

Great. "You want me to be your guest? Where?"

How much longer until they show up?

Amalia shrugged. "They are about ten minutes out, if you'd like to know."

What the hell?

"I know. I hear that a lot."

Kalinda's eyes widened as she stared at Amalia.

Amalia tapped her temple with a long red fingernail. "I read these."

Well, isn't that—

Kalinda cut off her thought, afraid Amalia would still be snooping. "What does being your guest mean, and why would the Trinity have need of me?"

Lennox cocked his head to the side. "Well, to be on the Council, of course."

How about no? Dammit!

Amalia chuckled. "You can't stop your thoughts any more than you can stop the breeze. But we are getting ahead of ourselves. Lennox, darling, you always cut too quickly to the chase when diplomacy would be better. She hasn't even heard our offer. Let's move this conversation, shall we?"

Lennox inclined his head to Amalia. "Of course. Yon?"

Thunder boomed so loudly, Kalinda couldn't make out what Silva tried to say, only reading her lips.

No! Run!

Well, duh, Silva. But I can't run, now, can I?

Her head hurt. Correction, everything hurt. Was it possible that gums could disintegrate? Kalinda checked to find out, but her gums were still there, even if sore. She groaned and shook her head, trying to clear the cobwebs, but that only made it worse.

"Give yourself some time. The first phase is always the hardest." Amalia's voice was soothing.

That was the understatement of the year. Kalinda took the advice though, letting her body rest—on a sofa?—on the soft material under her. She sank into the cushion, taking big deep breaths and mentally taking stock of all her body parts. It felt weird to do so, but she wasn't sure if she was coming or going. After a few minutes, she finally opened her eyes.

She was surrounded by decadence and sitting on a couch with deep gold cushions and red pillows. A matching chaise was across from it with a red lacquer table in between. The walls of the room were white and covered in glowing, golden words she couldn't hope to read, but as she kept staring at them, something deep inside rejoiced.

She stood, slowly, and walked toward the walls, ignoring the Trinity standing in the room with her, and approached with one hand raised. The scrolling lettering was an odd mix of runes and written words similar to Sanskrit blended in between. One sentence stuck out.

Bransg micaloz.

She had no idea how she was able to read it or what it meant.

You know this.

It was the voice she'd heard inside the Chaos Realm. She jerked.

Do not fear me, child. We said we would be with you, the voice said.

Sure, and where were you when they scared the hell out of me and stole me from my store?

Sometimes, you need to be uncomfortable to grow. We will ensure you are not harmed. Trust us.

I trust no one.

You will.

"Who is she communicating with?"

"I don't know, Lennox. Her mind is blocked from me. It's a blank slate." Amalia's voice was filled with shock.

"Impossible," Lennox protested.

"And yet true. She is one of the Old Ones," Amalia argued.

Lennox hmphed. "We won't know until she is properly tested."

"We will get to that. Kalinda? That's your name, right?" Amalia finally addressed Kalinda directly.

Kalinda forced herself to look away from the lettering on the walls. Now that she looked, she saw *bransg micaloz* everywhere, and the words formed into recognizable patterns. *Protect light.*

"Yes," she answered after a moment.

"Please, sit. You've been through a lot," Lennox offered.

Are you still here? She was talking to spirits, in her head, but that was better than being alone. No way she was going to get in touch with Romano now, and her spell phone was God only knew where.

Always, the spirits alerted her. *Amalia will not read you within these walls where our words are written. She miscalculated.*

Sweet.

Now she sounded like Giuliana.

She took a seat across from Amalia, Yon, and Lennox on the couch and waited for them to begin. The sooner she could get the information and say no, the better.

Amalia spoke first. "Do you know what the Old Ones are?"

Kalinda shook her head. "I'd never heard the phrase, but then I'm not high on the magical level."

"Ah, but you are," Amalia replied. "The Old Ones were from before there were Enchanted Zones, or even the Pendulum Swing of the 1950s. While many don't understand this, magic has been around since the dawn of time, and humans have lost their connection with said magic over the millennia."

"But before the loss, there were nine families who housed the magic within their bloodlines. These families were Valdi, Scetto, Riordan, Olfader, Tigris, Dinah, Ashur, Aegis, and Vasilios," Yon continued. "Each family helped a particular form of magic sacred to their bloodlines, and from them, magic was passed on."

"The family heads are considered the Old Ones," Lennox finished.

They were like a circus act, starting and completing each other's sentences, and while it was all very fascinating, it didn't explain much to Kalinda. Obviously, none of those names were hers, and it sounded like they were a pretty big deal.

"Okay?" She wasn't seeing the link.

Amalia smiled. "It's a lot, so we won't explain it all. We were raised on this knowledge and have understanding of each of the family lines. It's the reason we have the FBMC, to group those with some semblance of the blood into Enchanted Zones."

Ah, so she had some connection so far off she couldn't even call it family. Got it. And?

"So where does that leave me and you wanting me on the Council?"

"The Old Ones are long gone, of course, but those who are closer to the bloodline have more strength in their magic, the levels. And those at the highest levels are closer to the Old Ones. And then there are others …"

Amalia's voice trailed off. She looked to Lennox, and he opened his hand. Fire, brilliant orange, yellow, and blue, danced in his palm and formed into a perfect circle with flames flickering upward. He let the ball dance over his fingers and grow before tossing it lightly. It hovered over the table between them. The heat pulsed and warmed Kalinda, close enough to almost burning but not quite.

"I am a Level 9, as are the rest of the Trinity, one step below all members of the National Council. We are born within this level, but there are times when some may change their power level when it is called for."

"They are called Ales, which means Chosen. Chosen are meant to be part of the Council and a counterpart to the Trinity," Yon explained.

The stared at her expectantly.

Yeah, no. Not even a little bit. She wasn't some Ales, Chosen, or whatever else they wanted to call her. Kalinda had a feeling that admitting it, or showing some interest in it, would just make them more interested in keeping her. She was just Kalinda, owner and operator of Kalinda's Katering, who was trying to go international with her baking skills and enjoyed occasionally helping others through her magic. That was her place in the world, and she liked it just fine.

What they were insinuating was more than she ever wanted to deal with. She remembered Zahara telling her she was powerful, but that didn't mean she had to do what they wanted her to do. She was just as well managing what she had. Most of the time, that seemed nearly too much, but she enjoyed it, loved it even.

No, she was not going to feed into this. "What happened to Giuliana and Silva?"

"They were successfully retrieved shortly after we left, and the wolves showed up in force. With her Alpha there, Giuliana was able to immediately come out of the spellwork you put her under. The Fae, well, we'll get to her another time. She shouldn't be here. You were more important," Yon answered.

And that right there was just another reason Kalinda would be giving a resounding no. Their lack of compassion meant she wanted nothing to do with them. They knew all of that and could have told her, and Silva was not someone who didn't belong here. None of them did, truly, and all of their lives had been ripped open under the sweeps by the FBMC.

It had ruined her life, her chance at marriage, and having a family. Finding she had magic also shook her foundation in believing anyone could really love her and stick by her. Her fiancé left the minute he knew she was one of *those people* and never looked back. Everything in her life, but her food, was a clusterfuck with this.

Magic wasn't always something of great pride for many of the people of Encantado, and too many of them hadn't received any help when they'd been torn away from the only family they knew just because they had a little magic.

Wrong answer.

"I'd like to leave, thank you. I enjoyed the story time, and it's wonderful knowing more about where magic came from, but none of this has anything to do with me."

"You're wrong, and there is too much to understand in just one day. We haven't explained everything to you. We understand this is a lot to take in. We've given you much to ponder and will talk about more later. Take your time before you make a decision," Amalia argued.

"I can take my time back home. I have a business to run and matters to attend to."

Lennox shook his head. "The business isn't necessary any longer, and a Mage Council member doing such work would be a conflict of interest in other business. Many would come to your establishment simply because of who you are and the chance to get closer to you."

They talked about completely changing her life, *again*, without a thought of what it meant to her.

"I said no."

Watercolor-face Man shifted. Kalinda thought she hated Yon the worst. The face shifting was creepy when he spoke. "And the privilege of being one of us is an honor and, while a choice, not one that can be said no to. We will let you rest on it and speak more on the morrow about who you are and what that means."

They stood as if she hadn't denied them multiple times. Kalinda leapt to her feet as well.

Not going to happen, dude. Not even a little bit.

Anger burned in her chest as her lungs filled with hot air and expanded, her skin tingling. She would not let anyone contain her. Not ever. Chills raced down her back and her fingers sweltered with power wrapping around them.

"*I said no.*"

Her voice was wrong, and the world ribboned with shades of black winking in and out. Gray fireballs, like in the Chaos Realm, pushed from her chest and hovered in front of her, spinning in a circle.

"Lennox!" Amalia screamed.

Lennox was already moving. "I see it."

"Let me go," Kalinda demanded.

The fireball Lennox had been controlling over the table expanded and contracted, turning into a snake of fire, and twisted its way around the circle of gray in front of her chest. Lennox was working, his fingers dancing fast enough to blur, and Kalinda wrenched forward, pulled by the fire she'd taken from him, but she jerked back, staying on her feet.

Help me!

The gray fireballs spread out, making Lennox's fire grow before shooting out toward the Trinity. They stood shoulder to shoulder, Yon and Amalia now working just as fast as Lennox.

"Sleep," they whispered in unison.

Rest, child. You're not yet ready to control this.

I can't stay here. I can't. Please.

He's coming. Trust us.

Who?

But they didn't answer before the world faded.

She was really tired of falling asleep like this.

CHAPTER *Seven*

She was gone.

After getting to Kalinda's shop and finding Silva and Giuliana literally foaming at the mouth, Romano figured Kalinda would be hiding somewhere out of her need to run from the stress of her changing magic. He didn't think he'd be able to think of anything else but the picture Silva and Giuliana struck: damn near half-clothed, sweaty and ready to go yet trying to fight anything in their path. It wasn't until he realized he couldn't smell Kalinda anywhere and traces of powerful magic over it that he realized their anger was because they hadn't been able to protect her.

"I'm sorry," Giuliana said for the umpteenth time. He loved the girl, but he was two seconds from punishing her like he would his men. But he'd been under the control of Kalinda's magic before and he knew how powerful it was.

"Explain again what happened," Dominic ordered. He'd brought extra men with him when Romano told him Kalinda needed them, just in case, and it was a good thing he did.

"We were eating the test batches of Kalinda's cake when all I could think about was mating to the nearest male I could find. There were no males, obviously, and that caused a bit of an issue. By the time I even sensed the Trinity was here, it was too late. I was too far gone, and even though I was fighting to get back and help, I couldn't do much. The Fae did better."

Romano turned on the small Fae Kalinda employed to take care of her shop. Silva nodded. "It's like she said. I was able to sense them faster and tried to react but couldn't. I tried to tell Kalinda to run, but she couldn't get away. Her magic is even more powerful than it was the day with the Leo, I was unprepared to handle it."

Why the hell would the Trinity come for Kalinda? Zahara said the Council would check on her, but that didn't mean the Trinity. They never came for anything unless there was war brewing between shifters or magical factions.

"Scenters, head out and see which direction they traveled. One of the Trinity is a phaser, but he leaves traces when he ports. We may be able to pick up something," Dominic called out.

While any shifter generally had a good nose, scenters worked exclusively on tracking and had a highly developed sense of smell. If anyone could pick up anything, it would be them, but Romano was not optimistic.

"I'm calling Zahara. She may know more than we do."

It took a few minutes of haggling her price, but the witch said she'd be on her way, and Romano was left to wait. His wolf pounded against the confines of his cage, wanting to get out and search for Kalinda himself. There was nothing either of them could do. The Council Headquarters was on the outskirts of Encantado, near the portal into the city. They were also shielded by a ward tougher than Fort Knox, and no one could get in unless invited.

It took some time, but the scenters eventually came back after finding the signature of the phase in the direction of the Council Headquarters, like Romano had expected.

"Fuck," Dominic cursed. "Even Arturo didn't want to trifle with the Council if he didn't have to, but I may need his help getting an audience with them."

"And it just keeps getting better."

"Oh, just you wait." Zoey's eyes blazed with anger. "You let my best friend be taken. You're going to die."

Romano groaned. Zoey didn't get vindictive or mean very often, but she was ridiculously headstrong and stubborn when it came to her family and friends. He'd have to protect his balls while he slept if he didn't bring Kalinda home, and fast.

Giuliana must have thought the same thing because she slumped in her chair, hands to her head, and whimpered. "Can I just tell her it was all Romano's fault?"

"No. I'm throwing you both under the bus. It's not going to be *my* fault."

"What great leadership we have," Giuliana mumbled.

"The better to ruin your world with, my dear."

Zahara arrived before there could be any more back and forth between them, her face paint vibrant and her white dress swishing around her ankles. Bells and coins tinkled together with each step from jewelry around her ankles, and she was barefoot, red paint on the soles of her feet.

"They have claimed her."

"No, they *took* her," Dominic clarified.

Her eyes swung to the *Capo di tutti Capi*. "For the Council, that is one and the same. They have been looking to fill their ranks since one of them died, and she has the power to do it."

"I'm not leaving her with them," Romano promised.

Zahara sucked a breath through her teeth and rolled her eyes. "Did I say there was not a way? I only stated what happened."

Hearing there was a way outside of diplomacy that could take however long, Romano perked up. "And what would that be?"

Zahara shook her head as if Romano was completely slow. "Moon-bite."

"Well, shit." Giuliana was not helping. Not even a little bit.

"The full moon isn't for two weeks. There isn't any way I'd let her stay here for that long and *hope* I could give her the bite."

The moon-bite marked the one receiving as a mate to the wolf who gave the bite. It was done under the full moon, and even if the man didn't believe the chosen woman was his mate, his wolf made the decision and it was accepted.

But was he ready for that? Okay, he wanted her, and he knew she was his, but he'd always struggled with matings. Most wolves didn't understand why he was that way, but they didn't have his parents or his upbringing. Didn't have to watch as a mate-bond forced two people together who didn't love each other until … finally … they tore apart.

Would he be destined to the same result when Kalinda desperately fought him at every turn?

A moon-bite was never wrong, and it was what Dominic had used to have Zoey as his recognized mate and get out of the pre-arranged marriage with Fabiana Bianchi, but his hadn't been a true bite.

"The Council will recognize such an important part of your customs or face backlash from the shifter community, which is larger in many ways than pure magic groups. By claiming her as such, you can be by her side while she is with them," Zahara explained.

"That doesn't bring her home."

"One step at a time, Romano. If you are there with her, the chances of her leaving are much higher than her being there alone with no protection."

"I can't wait for two weeks to get there—if they give an audience that fast in the first place—and let that be the only way I can get to her."

Dominic snapped his fingers. "I may have an idea, but I need to speak with Arturo first. Can you give a few minutes, Zahara?"

"It's on your dime, and I charge extra for wasting my time."

"Of course."

Once the witch was gone, Romano turned to Dominic. "What is it?"

"Hold on."

Dominic was already getting on his phone, and Romano found his wolf wanted to get out. It needed to run, fight, and tear through anything to get to Kalinda. She must have been terrified, fighting with everything she had to get out. In the time he'd known her, he learned she didn't like to be trapped. Maybe he should have paid more attention. If he had come with her to make sure she was getting her job done in her shop instead of believing having free rein of pack lands would be enough, this may not have happened. Romano would have come with more men.

Instead, he'd overestimated the allure of pack lands and maybe of himself. For three days he'd given her space, but was there, a quiet protector she could rely on if she needed. But she'd never asked, not once. She moved around his home, cooking, cleaning, scribbling notes on ideas and putting them neatly on the bedside table of the guestroom for later use. Her mind was always working through some way to make Kalinda's Katering better, to better assist her clients, or coming up with new recipes so she was one step ahead of the competition. He'd never seen someone work so hard.

He respected her fire and *liked* who she was more and more. Now, she'd been taken, and he had to get her back one way or another. The idea of taking her as a mate was permanent, and he wasn't sure how to think about it.

Sure, he loved how her body was, her mind, even the way she fought him at every turn. She was so serious he needed to pick at her just to give her something to lighten up about. But he knew a life with him in the world he lived in wouldn't be easy. Though the Lombardi Pack had changed a lot of their ways, they were still violent and bloody. Sometimes, people had to die, and they were the ones to do it.

Since his promotion, Romano was Dominic's right hand, and what job Dominic didn't do, Romano did. Kalinda didn't live life like that. She was light and beauty, a businesswoman and entrepreneur carving out her place in the world. As his mate, things would be different.

Yes, she'd still have her business, but if they were at war, or there were problems, how she ran her business may change, if she could even be there in person. Serving and being in the middle of potentially dangerous situations would not be accepted.

Romano had a feeling telling Kalinda any of that would only start a war he'd be desperate to win. But did he want her? God, yes. He would never deny that, and his wolf howled at the chance of even getting her. But moon-bite? That was permanent on a level he hadn't even thought they could get to yet.

"Can it be done now?" Dominic clenched his phone to his ear. "Good. Whatever it takes, and I'll owe you one ... yes, I know what that means. I know better than anyone."

When he hung up, Romano shook his head. "I will owe him one, not you. I didn't mean for you to give that sort of promise, and you have Zoey to think of. Pups."

"It is what it is. You saved my life, and now I'm helping you. End of story. Zahara!"

Zahara poked her head back into the room. "I'm right here. It's not like I didn't hear it all anyway. And you should tell him what you promised to give in return for this favor. He deserves to know."

"That is pack business, where it will remain."

"Dominic—"

"I *said* end of story."

The power of an Alpha permeated his words, sending shards of pain into Romano's head. He stumbled under the pressure, and Giuliana, already weak from Kalinda's magic and fighting it, passed out on the floor. Romano nodded his head, exposing his neck in a sign of submission.

He and Dominic, well, their bond went deeper than perhaps blood could have ever made them. It wasn't just about Dominic pulling him out of the Chaos Realm. He'd been there, tearing through ranks and proving himself when Dominic's world had turned to shit.

When his mother dishonored their pack and walked away from her mate and never looked back. Romano had been thrown into a maelstrom, and the upstart Made Wolf helped him get through. He'd follow Dominic to the end of the earth.

Even thinking about the way the pack had dealt with them, the pity in their gaze pissed him off. His mother had forsaken her wolf and family. Something must be wrong with any children from someone like that, right? Dominic never saw it that way; he just accepted Romano and walked beside him.

Would Kalinda do the same, or would she be like his mother, denying what the wolf told them? He wasn't sure, but he didn't have the time to examine that fear too closely. Saving her was paramount.

"Now," Dominic explained, "Arturo is owed a boon because he exposed what Benedict was doing with Ottavio. This boon can be used to request an immediate audience for assistance. He will use it for the Lombardi Pack to meet with the Council about Kalinda with her presence as a stipulation, along with yours."

"You are smart, young Alpha," Zahara complimented.

"Are we planning to snatch her?" Romano could completely get behind an idea that involved him releasing his wolf to go crazy.

"We wouldn't make it out of there alive. They would never allow enough wolves in there to fight them, and their level of magic would be too high. No, what you're going to do is bite Kalinda as soon as you get her close enough to you. The bite must be enough to produce a possibility of her shifting by the next full moon."

"That could kill her!" Just the thought of hurting Kalinda made Romano's chest seize.

"Yes, but it also makes her your mate and will give you time until the full moon to do a moon-bite. As a mate, and in danger of not surviving the bite, you will have to be there for assistance." Zahara stated it like a foregone conclusion, and Romano didn't know if he was ready to accept it.

"It is a good plan and just may work. You will just have to get within biting distance," Dominic explained.

Yes, it may be the only way, but allow her to face potential death? A Born Wolf, like Romano, didn't have to worry about what the First Shift would do to him. They were born to be shifters and may even spend the first few months of their lives back and forth between pup or human baby as their bodies grew and got used to the changes.

A Made Wolf was much different and not as easy to navigate. Most Made Wolves didn't survive through their First Shift. Zoey had survived, thanks to a no-shift potion made for her by Warlock Cyrus, but the strength of Dominic's bite still gave her amplified sight, hearing, and smell. She was nearly as strong as some wolves without the ability to shift. She was a special case.

Kalinda would have no access to the no-shift potion and would face the danger of not making it through shifting.

"And what about her magic shifting so much? Will that cause a problem?" Because Romano didn't want to add unnecessary danger.

"We don't know, but it may be our only shot. If we wait until trying to see them on the full moon, even with Arturo's boon, we may risk them not even letting her close if they know what could happen. Hell, they might even know it's a risk now. We have to take what we can get."

"Fuck!" Romano wished he had an enemy in front of him, his gun in his hand, or claws to rip through anything right now. This entire situation was getting out of control, and they still didn't know what the Viscount Pride had to do with it, even after looking into it for three days. They needed to know why the pride was on Kalinda's trail in the first place and who put them up to it. The obvious answer was the Council, but no evidence led to that.

What was happening to Kalinda? Why did the Viscount Pride try to take her and what did they know? Why did the Council want her on the team? And would she survive?

There were too many questions and not enough answers. With everything that was happening lately, Romano and the others were forced to be reactive instead of proactive. It left them making bad decisions.

Dominic approached Romano and placed a heavy hand on his shoulder. "I will be right there with you, and we know how strong Kalinda is. She'll survive because she's too stubborn to die. She's that sort of woman. She's got a core of steel, and if she had been a wolf, she'd be warrior-class. Trust that."

Would he trust it if it were Zoey? But there was no reason to ask that. Dominic had risked it when he bit her at the catering event. He couldn't have known she would survive or have access to the no-shift potion. He'd risked it all to claim her and could have lost her too.

The last few months had been a whirlwind of revelations the pack hadn't gotten used to yet. The community they'd built for the children of District 17 was thriving, and business was as well, but a run-in with other shifters or the Council could upset the delicate balance.

Benedict's betrayal had put a bad stain on the Council as a whole, and perhaps taking Kalinda would be a way of storing their defenses. Romano taking a mate who was a mage could mean anything for the children they'd have. The Council was more interested in tipping the scales in their favor. Having Kalinda under their control would be a strategic move.

"Well, I can't have you one-upping me by risking how you claimed your mate. I'm going to claim a mate, and she's going to be a Council member. Top that!"

"You forget my mate is an Alpha's mate. She rules anyway," Dominic said loftily.

"Yeah, but is she a Council member with the Trinity personally wanting her? I win."

"Zoey? Come here for a minute."

Zoey, questions marring her features, came to stand beside her mate, and Dominic moved her close to Romano. Vegetation outside the window exploded and twisted until Romano jumped back away from Zoey.

"Low blow," Romano argued.

"I win. My mate is the Alpha bitch *and* can make shit grow like the ooze. I win."

Romano blinked. "You bitched at me for the fertilizer thing, and now you link it to green turtles in the sewer? Classic."

"I officially hate both of you. This growing thing since the portals have been popping up is not cool. At all." Zoey stomped her foot, and it was … adorable.

This was a jest, just to lighten the mood, and Romano was thankful Dominic could help him at a time like this.

Romano would find a way. Come hell or high water, Kalinda would survive. There was no other option.

They could deal with the mating situation, and the Viscount Pride, afterward.

CHAPTER *Eight*

Romano dressed carefully in a black suit, tailor-made to stretch across his chest, stark white shirt, and thin black tie. His shoes were Italian leather, and he made controlled chaos of his hair before strapping on a gold watch and diamond cufflinks. He tucked a singular red silk napkin in his breast pocket and put on his ring that symbolized him as a Made Man and Born Wolf. The howling wolf was nestled in a crescent moon and decorated with brilliant ruby eyes. The ring matched the tattoo across his bicep.

He'd never gone to the Council Headquarters, so he pulled out all the stops to go for Kalinda. It wasn't every day a man proposed by bite to a woman who might or might not want to rip his balls off when she found out.

Each step was heavy out of his now quiet home—the essence of Kalinda not as vibrant now that he knew she wasn't safe—and headed to his car to pick up Dominic. What Romano found instead was Giuliana, dressed in a fashionable blood-red dress and matching heels, diamonds dripping from her throat and ears. At the end of the day, though she was with the Lombardi Pack, she was Arturo Moretti's niece and commanded that respect.

She waited next to a sleek sedan and opened the door for him with a bowed head. "*Capo.*"

He accepted her direction and climbed into the car and waited for her to get in. It seemed they all were going to stand in ceremony today to meet the Council. It only enhanced his pride in his pack and what they were willing to do for each other. Romano still didn't know what Dominic had promised, but the fact Dominic had done it meant a lot.

They arrived at Dominic's home moments later and both Dominic and Zoey emerged. If Dominic was a storm brewing with his slate-gray suit and matching accessories, Zoey was pure light in all white. She wore flats instead of heels, in deference to her stomach, but Romano wondered why she was coming. When they got in the car, he stared pointedly at Zoey.

She waylaid him, of course, and spoke first. "Shut up before I stab you."

He blinked. "But I didn't say anything."

"Yeah, well I'm still mad at you, and since you oafs can't deal with things any other way than violence, I figured I could practice on you. Want to show me where the carotid artery is and the right pressure to puncture it?"

Romano choked on a laugh. "When did you get bloodthirsty?"

"When a wolf started growing in my stomach. Still not answering the question."

Zoey blinked, tears pooling in her eyes and Romano was at a loss. Danger, guns, violence, he knew how to deal with all that, but a crying woman made him uncomfortable. What was he supposed to do with her? Thump her back and go kill something? Seemed like a good option.

His mother never cried. She growled and spat insults before stalking off to be gone for days on her own. He hadn't really learned to deal with women until he'd gotten older and took a few knocks learning the ropes—crying was not something he'd mastered.

Dominic saved him and placed one hand on his mate's stomach and his other arm around her. He pulled her close, and she buried her nose in his neck, breathing deeply. It was an intimate moment. It should have been private, so Romano turned his head away.

"She will be fine, *mi amore*. There is no man I'd trust more than Romano to protect her."

"I know but," *sniffle*, "what if they hurt her?" *Muffled sob.* "Or she *dies?*"

Her last word was said on a wail, and Dominic, never breaking a sweat, pulled his mate closer. "Then I would reach into death to pull her back if it made you happy."

"What if she hates me for tying her up in this?"

"No one hates sunshine, Zoey."

"You do, first thing in the morning."

"I don't hate it. I'd just rather be in you in the morning."

"But she's not going to be very happy with me."

"And then she'll be fine, you know this."

The conversation made absolutely no sense to Romano, but it helped Zoey. She hiccupped softly into Dominic's neck as they pulled away and headed out of pack lands.

Romano cleared his throat. "Will anyone else come with us?" *Take the hint, Dominic. Why is Zoey here?*

"We thought showing a face of comradery would help more. Just you, Giuliana, Zoey, and me. There will be a car following us, but they will remain outside awaiting our return."

The rest of the trip was made in silence, and Romano looked out the window for most of it. The areas the Moretti and Lombardi Packs owned were green and more upscale now.

But he barely saw the apartment complex building, the community center, or the faces of businesses opening back up within pack lands as they drove. None of it mattered as much as getting to Kalinda.

Each mile felt like ten as they traveled from one side of Encantado to another. By the time they reached the manicured drive leading into headquarters, Romano wanted to rip at his shirt neck and throw his tie on the floor. Her refrained, barely, from doing either. Instead, he decided to leave his weapons in the car. Besides, his teeth were all he needed. He worked on having a partial shift ready to allow his teeth to extend when the time came. Partial shifting was something easier for a Born Wolf to do but still required some concentration when not in a heightened emotional state.

They went up the lit drive that was darkened by the large willow trees on either side that blocked some of the early evening sun. Wards danced along the lights—a warning system for those inside and defensive spells for anyone coming who wasn't allowed to come this way.

They had an audience, but the searching magic still crept along Romano's skin, making his hair raise on end. After a few more minutes, they reached a tall, gilded wrought iron gate. It opened automatically as they approached and let them go through. In the center of the circle drive in front of the mansion was a marble fountain of a woman holding fire in one hand, the ground raising beneath her feet, water streaming from the other, and her hair frozen in a fierce wind.

"You think we need any more reminders of their magic?" Dominic scanned the fountain with a critical eye.

"Maybe gargoyles?"

Zoey snorted. "They have those too. Look at the top of the place."

Sure enough, watching gargoyles turned their heads as the cars parked.

"Maybe a talking lion's head on the door?"

"I don't know if it talks, but ..."

Romano was officially done with what-ifs. The four of them got out of the lead car and headed for the front door. Before they could knock, the lion head opened its mouth wide.

"Welcome, Dominic, *Capo di tutti Capi* of the Lombardi Pack, Zoey, your mate, Romano, your *Capo*, and Giuliana, your Enforcer. We will see you now."

"Romano," Dominic hissed, "shut up next time we go somewhere new, okay?"

"It's a puss—"

"Don't you say—"

"We eat those." Romano smiled as he got the last word, canines sharp and big. The lion roared but wisely closed its mouth.

"See?"

"Can I call him Puss? Like, you know, that orange cat on the movies with the big eyes. All it needs is a hat."

"I'm going to kill you myself," Dominic growled, but he couldn't completely hide his grin.

No point in showing the Council they were afraid. As the door swung open, Dominic and Zoey entered first, heads held high, with Romano and Giuliana taking up the rear. The door closed behind them, encasing them in momentary darkness, and Romano resisted the urge to growl.

This was not natural dark, but magic dark, and he never liked it after being in the Chaos Realm. Every muscle ticked and contracted, ready for battle from any direction. A soft growl permeated the air and grew until Romano recognized his Alpha's call. He blinked, and the darkness faded.

"What the hell is wrong with y'all?" Giuliana stared at them a moment.

"They've been in the Chaos Realm. The wards at the door mark those who have. It is for the protection of the home."

Romano looked up to find a woman standing at the top of the twin staircases on either side of the foyer. "We didn't come with a threat."

"No, but the realm does. It's good to know who has been there and who hasn't."

"Will we be meeting in here, or do you have somewhere more comfortable in mind?"

The woman tilted her head. "You are the Alpha Dominic. Quite a specimen."

"*My* specimen," Zoey warned, her lip wrinkling in a warning growl.

"Ah, and his magic-blood mate."

Giuliana and Romano shifted forward, sensing their Alpha's hackles rising.

"Is there a point to this game?"

Lennox smile sharply. "It's a dance, Dominic. A dance to make you understand who the leaders are."

Thunder clapped, loud, snapping through the room, and when Romano opened his eyes, they were somewhere much different than the foyer. It could only be a sunroom—solarium he thought he'd heard Zoey call it when she had one built for the baby—and the doors were flung wide open. The Trinity, Romano guessed, sat in the center, Kalinda next to them asleep, and seats were across from them.

"What's wrong with her?" Romano was already moving forward before the woman could answer.

"Ah, ah, ah."

An invisible wall stopped him short of reaching Kalinda, keeping him from taking her into his arms. He could see her pulse jumping in her throat, but he didn't like the fact she wasn't awake.

"You may not touch a Council member without their express permission."

He was really getting tired of the woman. Like, want-to-eat-her-in-the-bad-way tired.

"My name is Amalia, and this is Lennox," she indicated a white-haired man, "and Yon."

Dominic didn't incline his head, but his tone showed deference. "The pleasure is mine. We set this meeting to discuss Kalinda and what is going on. We expect her to be *present* for the conversation."

"She is present. You see her here."

Okay, replace Amalia with Lennox for the to-be-eaten category.

Dominic growled. "You know what we meant. We are not here for games."

"Oh, we agree. Kalinda is very important to us." Lennox looked so smug, it took all of Romano's willpower not to use the little bastard as a toothpick. "You see, who she is to the world is important, as is the prestige she will bring to the Encantado Mage Council. No one else will have an Ales in their midst. As you can see for yourself, she is fine."

"I want to hear her say it herself," Romano argued.

"I am speaking to your Alpha, *Capo*, not to you."

Nope, he *really* didn't like Lennox. Nor the proprietary hand he placed on Kalinda's leg. His wolf went crazy, and he growled before he could stop himself.

"Romano …" Kalinda whispered, but he heard it.

He slammed into the invisible wall. "I'm here."

"She's reacting to him," Amalia whispered. She should have known they'd hear her with their heightened hearing, no matter how low she talked.

Kalinda slumped over again, and claws burst from Romano's hands. He could barely keep his wolf in check.

"Look at me, Kalinda. Let me see those beautiful eyes."

Romano barely recognized his own voice, but Dominic didn't interfere. Instead, he stood at Romano's side, giving his support.

"I want to know what is wrong with her. She's been appointed as a ward of the Lombardi Pack and is very special to my mate who has come here, *with child*, to check on her friend."

Dominic's words may have been nice, but the threat was razor sharp.

Amalia looked to Lennox before Yon inclined his head. "We can't wake her."

Dominic didn't speak again and lifted one brow.

"She became … agitated and lashed out when we brought her here. We only put her to sleep to protect her. She hasn't awakened, even long after the spell wore off. It was set for a few minutes at best."

"She's in there. Let me touch her; I know what to do." The Three Stooges looked at each other again, and Romano hit the wall. "It's not like I can carry her out of here and run, can I? Let me help her."

The douche in the eat category nodded stiffly, and the wall disappeared. Romano lunged forward and scooped Kalinda into his arms.

She smelled of chocolate and vanilla, the ingredients she'd used to make her cakes, and that same old magic he couldn't quite place. Her heart pounded strong against his chest, and he traced her pulse with his lips.

"Come on, baby. Don't keep me worried like this."

Her hands twitched against him, but that was all. Still, he'd gotten through.

"I know. You need more. You're hiding, but I'm here. Follow me."

He didn't know why he said it, but he could only use what he remembered from Zahara. He may not have had the same magic, but he could use his essence of the wolf. He reached out to Kalinda with his wolf, letting the power rub over her as he curled around her. His wolf whimpered and licked over her skin. The human side of him followed, using his tongue to trace a heated path over her neck and toward her ear.

"Don't be mad at me, okay?"

It would be the best he could do. Her fingers clenched into his shirt. He wasn't sure if it was a warning or a need for help, but he knew he was moving in the right direction to bring her back.

Her heat was hotter as he nipped her earlobe and kissed his way over her jaw. He angled his body the best he could to hide the movement from the others, but he couldn't forget they were there.

"I claim you," he whispered against Kalinda's skin.

His teeth punctured her skin as he bit deep, sucking against the blood that flowed and using his tongue to soothe the pain. With his saliva, he would be able to heal it, but it would be sore. He disengaged his teeth and just used his tongue, closing his lips over the wound as her arms came up and around him.

"No. Stop what you're doing," Lennox ordered.

Fierce triumph surged through him. His. She was his. *Too late, assholes.*

"He's *marked* her!" Amalia screamed.

Power pulsed a moment before Romano was thrown back, ripping him away from Kalinda and sending him careening into the wall next to the door they'd entered. Thick smoke from cracked mortar burned his eyes, and he gasped, his breath knocked out of him.

A howl tore through his stupor enough to get him focused, and Giuliana crouched in front of him, teeth and claws bared.

Dominic stood at the forefront, pushing Zoey behind him as he faced off against the Trinity. "You would strike one of mine?"

Alpha power swelled into the room, pressing cement blocks down on Romano's chest as he coughed to breathe.

"He claimed her! He had no right!" Amalia's voice was like nails on a chalkboard. "He was only supposed to help her."

Did she screech? The pounding in his head told him she did. Romano forced himself to sit up. This could turn deadly, and Kalinda wasn't safe.

"I only did what I could to bring her back. She is tightly tied to certain emotions and sensations. If you dipshits saw, I tried to be nice and easy at first, but my girl likes it rough." Romano coughed but managed a grin at the Three Douches.

Taking Giuliana's outstretched hand, he got to his feet and brushed off the specks of destroyed wall. Yeah, he'd feel that in the morning.

A moan stopped them all from saying anything further. "Romano?"

Kalinda's eyes opened, and she blinked a few times before frantically searching the room. When her gaze rested on him, every bone in her body went liquid and she relaxed. "You're here."

Damn, if that didn't do things to him on a level he couldn't describe. Clearing his throat before his voice cracked like a pubescent teen, he spoke. "Told you. Can't get rid of me that easily."

She looked up at him from the seat. Only at him. She sounded dazed and angry. "I want to go home."

Romano looked to Dominic, who shook himself enough to speak normally. "We're done here." There was a bite to his tone as he addressed the Trinity. "You struck one of my wolves who offered you help. As of now, Kalinda is a member of the Lombardi Pack and needs her pack to survive her First Shift. Any further discussion of whether she chooses to join the Council will have to wait until then."

"Out of the question. We have access to the best healers in the lands, and we will make sure she receives the no-shift potion as well. She will *not* be a wolf," Lennox promised with a little too much disdain in his voice.

"She is my *mate*, and Magic Law states a mate bond is sacred. This isn't a situation where she was forced to turn by a random bite."

"It is a random bite by someone who wanted her power," Lennox countered.

"I don't want her for her power. I want her because she's Kalinda."

Romano said the words to the Trinity, but he was looking at her. Their gazes locked as he took a step forward. "She has a choice in joining the Council, and that will wait until you can explain to us exactly what that means, but *first*, she is my mate, and that takes precedence." He put heavy emphasis on the word "us." She wasn't alone in this.

Dominic's voice boomed through the air. "Denying a pack member's claim to his mate means turning your back on all shifters who gave sovereignty to the Council to be part of the Enchanted Zones and live freely. Remember, our kind are not ruled by the same laws of magic."

Romano had never head of that, but Dominic's words rang true and loud.

Yon narrowed his eyes at Dominic. "She isn't permitted to leave until she understands what turning down a Council position means, as that is *our* law. But in deference to your customs, her mate can remain with her until her First Shift and the choice she will have to make." Yon grimaced as if the words were distasteful to him.

"Hello? Can everyone stop talking about me like I'm a piece of furniture and you're trying to decide which room you're going to put me in?" Kalinda snapped. "I don't want to be on the Council. End of story."

Lennox, the smug bastard, never looked at Kalinda but only at Romano as he spoke. "Turning down a Council appointment is not a viable option, as we've told you. But perhaps I should clarify. You may refuse the appointment and the controls therein, but to do so would mean your gifts are dangerous to us. We learned that with one who said no and caused irreparable damage. She is alive to atone for it, and for no other reason."

"I don't have time for games. Say what you are trying to say," Dominic raged.

"He's saying Zahara was the mage who said no, and the only reason she is still alive is because she is doing work to make up for what she did. And if Kalinda says no, she dies," Zoey clarified.

"Ah, and they say an old dog can't learn new tricks," Lennox jeered.

Yeah, I'm killing you the minute I get Kalinda clear. And I'm going to enjoy *it so much.*

So. Fucking. Much.

CHAPTER *Nine*

Romano wasn't going to sit there and let them pull the group apart. The Council knew just what they were doing. They wanted to keep him there with Kalinda— separated from his pack and Alpha—and beholden to their magic and spells he couldn't hope to break. Staying here would only ensure they'd keep Kalinda right where they wanted her and under their control.

That didn't change the fact the Council had the upper hand and they *were* trying to get her away from them. He never got the story from Zahara about how she'd escaped the Council, and from their hint, she was paying for it in some way. He was sort of really pissed his wolf tried to eat her and still got uncomfortable when she was around.

Kalinda wasn't holding on. Trapped on the chair with him unable to get to her, she lashed out again, slamming into an invisible all.

"I *want* to go home. You can't choose this for me."

"You're a child, but soon you'll learn. Sleep."

Romano roared, feeling helpless he couldn't do anything as he watched Kalinda slump over again when Lennox waived his hand in her direction.

"You piece of shit. You couldn't wake her last time, and then you do it *again*? What the fuck is wrong with you?"

"Romano," Dominic warned.

Romano was over it. Over them. Over their heavy handedness. Over. All. Of. It. "She doesn't deserve to be treated like this, and all you're doing in ensuring she won't ever choose you. You're making sure she chooses death because she'd rather do that than take what you're force feeding down her throat."

Lennox's gaze was hard. "Do you think *any* of us had a choice? Do you think being high-level mages means we can live life any way we see fit? We have responsibilities too, or we could be dangerous. She's created situations, though small, because she cannot control her magic. You can't deny that. And there are those who would want to use her against us as well."

"The Viscount Pride," Romano guessed. "I wonder how they knew about her in the first place." Yeah, his tone was sarcastic, but he didn't give a shit.

"What's done is done. She turned an entire pride into an orgy, and by the time we came for her, she had two more locked into her magic. Without control, she could cause entire wars or manipulate people without even trying," Amalia explained.

"Her places as an Ales is at our side, it is what it is," Yon finished.

"There is nothing to fear by allowing her to come home to her pack and heal until after her First Shift. You *do* understand she was bitten by a Born Wolf and is, by your definition, a Level-9 mage?"

Thank God Dominic had thought of that, and his words were enough to give the Council pause. Shifters had decided to give sovereignty to the National Council in order to live publicly and have protections against humans who wanted to try to hunt them. It was stupid, but it happened. Instead of all-out war, non-mages—paranormals like vampires and shifters—agreed to follow mage rule if their rites were respected by the Council. For shifters, those were things like mage-bites, shifting phases, and pack-specific needs their animals called for.

A Born Wolf could change mages and non-mages, but typically, non-mage humans didn't survive the transitions, as was nearly the case for Dominic. But it also meant the change, if completed, could give the surviving wolf extra power in specific regards. Dominic was nearly indestructible, something that helped him within the warrior class.

What Kalinda would be was anyone's guess.

Lennox gritted his teeth. "Exactly why she needs to stay here so we can monitor her."

"Can you perform the position of Alpha and call her wolf to heel when it's trying to rip its way out of her body because it's terrified?"

"She will not be a wolf at all when she is given the no-shift formula. None of that matters."

"And you can't give it to her without her choice. She isn't lucid right now, and she has to give her consent to take the potion. You know these laws."

Romano could see nothing Dominic said was getting through to them. They wanted Kalinda any way they could have her, and it didn't matter what rules they broke.

"Is this worth breaking ties with the shifter community?" Romano stood tall, his gaze directly on Lennox.

"I could ask the same to you, *wolf*. Is taking her, against what we're telling you, worth being excommunicated from Encantado?"

Fuck. Yes. She was his despite how it happened and his fears. He couldn't turn over his mate. But ... he had to think of his people too. The pups who lived safely within measure within the portal cities.

"Look, all we're asking for is twenty-eight days to work with her and teach her to be a wolf. To be with her at her shifting and see her through. No one is saying anything about her not joining the Council. We understand your warning that for her to say no is a death sentence. But she should *choose*."

"Some of us are not given a choice, Dominic. *He* took the choice away from her when he bit her without her consent," Amalia countered, looking pointedly at Romano.

Well, hell. She had them there. His wolf howled, wanting his mate but also confused about the emotions coursing through him. A shifter mate wasn't always about choice when the wolves were involved. Hell, he'd seen his own parents destroyed by what their wolves had chosen for them when they hadn't followed emotionally. Was he repeating the same mistake they had?

Was something wrong with his blood?

He didn't know, but he wasn't going to let them keep her. They could figure out the rest later. But what could he do? They stood against three of some of the most powerful mages in the world. Romano wracked his brain, trying to come up with anything. He was still separated from Kalinda, and she was groggy, going in and out of consciousness. At least she didn't seem as trapped in the Chaos Realm as before, but he needed to get his hands on her and get them out.

"Her place with the Council … what is it?" Romano was sick to death of being in the dark. "What does it mean for her to be an Ales?"

Amalia turned toward him. "It means she's the balance of the Trinity and, as such, must be with the Council. It means her bloodline is old enough to command great respect and responsibility to the magekind. She must be under strict guidance and the instruction of the Council and National Council to be safe. The rest is for her to understand."

They were back at square one. Romano still didn't see a way for them to come eye to eye when their positions were opposite sides of the spectrum. The Council cared about the magic and what it would mean for the mages, and the wolves, well, they just cared about Kalinda.

An impasse could only be handled by a fight to the bitter end or retreat by one side. But even with a retreat, he'd have to make sure they couldn't be followed. He needed a fucking barrier.

Holy. Shit.

"We're not here to fight, Lennox. That was never our intention."

Romano let Dominic keep arguing and inched closer to Zoey. Giuliana cut her gaze at him. Years of working together put them in good stead, and she slid forward. Wolves didn't stalk, instead using freeze frame movements like cats. They hunted as a pack. The loudest wolves weren't what their prey had to worry about—it was the silent ones who would kill them.

Giuliana moved forward, closer to her Alpha, and started arguing with Amalia too. With each passing moment, Romano was closer to Zoey, and he thanked his lucky stars the Three Stooges had chosen a solarium for the meeting place.

"Zoey," he whispered. She may not have shifted, but carrying a wolf pup made her sense of hearing much better than any human's. She twitched but otherwise made no outward show she'd heard him.

"I'm *really* going to need that need that poopourri stuff you can do. I'm talking Tarzan-in-the-jungle wild."

"Kalinda?"

"Giuliana will get her."

"*Yes*, we're wolves but …"

Romano didn't listen to the rest of Giuliana's words to Amalia. Her stressed "yes" was her way of telling him she heard him, and that's all that mattered. Dominic was right near his mate, and Romano caught him grabbing her hand.

Look likes it's all a go then.

"Game on, Zoey."

Romano grasped Zoey's other hand in his, and … felt nothing.

Well, that's a let dow—

Vines pushing through the ground. That's the only way he could describe how his blood flowed through his veins. Deep, moist earth separated under the strain of new life bursting through to the sun. His flesh tightened, pulled taut with magic, and his wolf howled, welcoming a new moon.

Zoey was *life*, pure and simple.

And in the background, nearly so quiet he almost didn't catch it, a pup yipped, laughter bubbling up around him.

Dominic, she's beautiful and so strong. Dude, you're having a girl! *This is going to be epic.*

A loud, fierce growl ripped him from the sensations he'd pulled from Zoey—his Alpha's call. Instantly, Romano was back in action, dragging Zoey close to his chest and keeping their hands glued together. All around them, plants and vines shot up, bursting through the windows and filling the solarium.

"Burn it, Lennox!"

Amalia really liked screeching, but Lennox listened, his hands working fast to create fireballs. He shot them at each plant, withering them, but another grew in its place. Giuliana slipped through the foliage, leaving her heels behind.

"Romano, you *so* owe me a new pair of Louis."

She snatched Kalinda up in her arms and raced back toward them. Romano looked for an escape and saw a rapidly closing hole in the wall.

"Let's go!"

Amalia sneered. "They're taking her. Yon, stop them."

"I can't. I'm grounded."

Whatever that meant, but it worked in their favor. The group rushed toward the window and leapt through.

Dominic curled around Romano and his mate the best he could, cushioning their fall to the hard-packed earth. Zoey cried out, but Romano couldn't feel pain through their connection, just a moment of fear.

"She's okay," he told his Alpha.

"Romano—"

"I wouldn't lie to you. I can feel her. More on it later. Let's get out of here first. I'm rubbing in your face what I just found out. You're dead, man. Dead, I tell you."

Outside, the carefully manicured rose bushes around the mansion were twisted and grotesque like a sideshow, massive thorns protruding into the air. The group slipped through, finding air pockets where they could.

"Fuck," Giuliana growled.

"You okay?"

"I'm fine. Thorn caught me. This growing shit is out of control."

"Well, couldn't exactly control it, but it worked."

"It got my ass, Romano."

Yeah, he'd totally laugh about that later.

Another thorn, wicked sharp, took a chunk out of his shoulder on the way past it. He growled his displeasure, pulling Zoey tighter to him. As much as he wanted to hold on to Kalinda, he couldn't risk letting go of Zoey's hand.

Giuliana huffed. "Think we can get to the car?"

"Yeah, about that ..."

Dominic was going to fucking kill him. There was the car they'd driven to the Council meeting, up in the air, with a huge sunflower blooming through it.

I mean, it is pretty ... I guess.

Zoey snorted. "I think the car looks better as a flowerpot."

Giuliana growled. "This is all your fault. Who thinks of shit like this?"

It freaking worked, and that's all they could hope for. It was ugly, and running through the thorns was not easy, but it was better than being trapped inside with the Council. There was no telling how long before they came after them.

So they ran ... and they didn't look back.

"You made a garden grow? Someone explain in a way that makes sense."

Though he may no longer be their Alpha, Arturo commanded respect and power. His dark hair with a silver streak was styled to immaculate perfection, and his golden gaze traced over Zoey.

"Is the Alpha's mate harmed?"

Zoey, who obviously had a death wish but didn't give a shit, went straight to the *Capo di tutti Capi* of the Moretti Pack and wrapped her arms around his waist. He looked awkward for a moment before he tapped her back soothingly.

"I'm fine, and your future grandchild is too."

Arturo raised his brows. "Grandchild?"

Zoey stepped back and rolled her eyes. "Who else? You've been a father to my husband, and he respects you as such. Of course, you'd be *nonno*."

Arturo didn't say anything for a moment and just watched Zoey. She took his stare head-on, holding her head high and her shoulders back. Dominic, Romano, and Giuliana were exhausted from running nearly ten miles before they thought it safe enough to call for backup, and then they continued to run to meet their ride. Zoey and Kalinda had rides the whole time, and Kalinda, thankfully, was back in Romano's bed. They all stood in his living room.

After a minute, Arturo nodded. "Does she know what this means, Dominic?"

"She didn't care, and neither did I. It is as Zoey says."

And there goes the neighborhood.

"You're totally screwed, Zoey. That was the worst decision ever. Didn't you see how he treated me?" Giuliana joked. "Oh my God! I'm going to have a little cousin. Sweet."

Romano raised his hand. "Oh, did I mention they're having a girl?"

Dominic whipped around. "How do you know this?"

"Felt it in the weird kumbaya circle. She is strong, too, and already feisty. Laughs like her mother, demands like her father."

He should have thought about it before he said it. Dominic's chest swelled with pride, but a stone-cold shutter slid down over his face. Arturo was no better, his elegant hand sliding into his pocket. Both gazes locked onto Zoey's stomach.

"I have accepted this child as my blood, and she will come as heir if there are no other children of my line as she is for yours," Arturo began.

"I hear and accept," Dominic answered.

"She will be protected in all things, and as heir, given place within both packs."

"I hear and accept."

"When she is marked, she shall be with the print of a Born Wolf and female Alpha."

Dominic sucked in a breath. "Is that possible? I'm a Made Wolf and her mother is a mage."

"Is she a pup in the womb?" Arturo clasped his hands in front of him.

"Yes," Zoey answered.

"Then she is a Born Wolf. However it may have happened, it is so."

"And a female Alpha?" Dominic clenched his fists at his sides.

"It is rare, but is has been done."

Dominic swallowed. "I hear and accept."

"Good. The Moretti Pack will join with the Lombardi Pack to protect the heir's home and Kalinda. The well-being of her mother is paramount."

"What if she wasn't an heir?"

Leave it to Zoey to ask the hard questions.

"I would have helped anyway, but now I'm willing to destroy the entire Council if it comes to that."

And he fucking meant it. It was in his eyes, the way his grin was more wolf than human. Arturo meant to face any battle that came their way, and Dominic matched him.

"The Council will be coming for Kalinda. They won't let this slight go," Dominic cautioned.

"Then so be it. I'll have men stationed here by the end of the day."

Dominic slid his hand in his pocket. "And what about Moretti lands?"

A harsh, predatory smile spread across Arturo's face. "There will be enough to keep us covered, but they won't be looking to come at us. Attacking my pack would only give me grounds to petition the National Council against them. Coming to help protect you is within my right. We will be here. And I'll send men to check out the Viscount Pride. They started this, did they not?"

"Yes, and faked an allergy to do it," Romano answered.

Arturo snorted. "It only worked because they were facing low-level mages. But we'll find out what their stake is too. Focus your men on the compound here. We'll cover outside and the perimeter."

Dominic nodded. "Agreed. Once we have everyone in place, we can meet to discuss measures and what we may have found in the morning. I have a feeling Romano may have a battle on his hands tonight."

"Oh?"

Romano shrugged at Arturo's questioning gaze. "I may have claimed Kalinda, and she won't be very happy with it."

"You are not your mother, Romano. You never have been. Get your mate underhand; that's all it takes."

Yeah, it was going to be that easy. Sure. Arturo left, and with him, Dominic, Zoey, and Giuliana. Until the next morning, the leaders had nothing else to do but coordinate their men. And Dominic made it plain that Romano's job was Kalinda for now.

Despite what Arturo said, Romano couldn't help but wonder. Sure, circumstances were different than when his mother was claimed by his father, and Born Wolves went by older laws at times than Made Wolves. But a wolf was a wolf, and they claimed when their wolf told them.

Romano understood and had been around magekind long enough to know they didn't understand wolves completely. Most of them feared the shifters, which was why no-shift had been created in the first place. The idea shifters went around just biting and changing everyone was a perpetuated fear. He wasn't certain where it had come from either. When wolves got rowdy at an event where mages were in attendance, most accidental bites weren't mate bites and didn't lead to automatic shifting.

But the fear was enough to send the masses running.

He could understand Kalinda. She'd been through enough upheaval in just the last few weeks. Adding the possibility of becoming a wolf and now having a mate would only add another layer to her world she viewed as full of shit.

Romano sighed. Yeah, having a mate was going to be the easiest thing in the world for her to fight against when death-by-Council, her new Level-9 power, and her position on the Council wasn't really much of a choice. And he'd just taken another choice away from a woman who loved freedom.

Not the best start to their mating.

CHAPTER *TEN*

Her head was pounding, and she was not in Kansas anymore. She recognized the room she was in, at least. *Always a silver lining, Kalinda. Just focus on that.* But she was *really* over waking up like this. Granted, this time she had much more pleasant company to look at, but she was pissed.

No. Pissed was an understatement.

Wrathful? Oh, that was good.

Seething? That might be a bit better.

Explosive? Got it in one!

Romano must have sensed it because his nostrils flared out, scenting the air, and grew still. "Kalinda …"

"My neck hurts, Romano. Care to tell me what that means?"

She knew, of course. She remembered how Zoey said she'd felt after she'd been bitten and favored her backside, of all places, for quite some time. And she'd had the no-shift potion within a short period to make sure she didn't turn wolfy. Kalinda had provided it at great expense to help her friend, of course, and now she found herself in the same predicament.

The fact she was in his bedroom without the potion already … in … her … hand told her she may have more than a little to deal with.

Romano sighed before rubbing his hand down his face. "You already know."

Nope. Not going to run from this. Not even a little bit. She was done taking everyone else's shit. She didn't choose any of this, and no one cared about *her* choice at every step.

"You mated me."

He nodded, and that sent her flying off the ledge directly into the deep end of molten lava. Everything *burned*. Acrid air met her nose, and heat pulsed off her scalp. Kalinda's skin was tight, pulling until it itched, and she clenched her teeth.

Yeah, he was sooooo dead.

"Did you even *once* think of how I'd feel?"

Romano ran rough hands through his hair, dislodging the dark strands across his forehead. "It's *all* I thought about, Kalinda. Did I know you'd be angry?" She snorted. "Yes. Did I know I'd have a mate who wasn't any more interested in being in my bed than having a root canal? Yeah, I knew that too. And I still did it to save her life."

Okay, to be fair, she didn't know what had happened when she was out in the crazy sphere, but still …

"Was there no other way? I mean, come on, how long have you been angling to get me in bed?"

Romano's eyes flashed and he seemed, she couldn't quite put a word to it … bigger? His shoulders were thrust back, his jaw jutted furiously, and his fists clenched at his side.

"If all I wanted was you in bed, I would have said so. If all I wanted was to make you come so many times you couldn't see straight and couldn't think unless it was about me, or for you to carry the taste of my possession for the rest of your life, I would have said that too."

Well. Damn. No, she wasn't going to let him change this around. "You know what I mean."

"Joining the Council or not is literally life or death, and I refused to let your death be on my hands. Be pissed if you want, but there it is."

"I didn't want any of this."

He flung his arms out wide, but she didn't back down, sitting up in the bed and matching him glare for glare.

"Too bad, baby. It's here, and we don't have any other choice."

"There is always a choice, Romano."

He growled. That sound didn't do anything to her lady bits. Okay, that was a lie.

"You know what, stop. Just stop. I get it. This has messed up every plan you've ever had with your life, the least of which was ever being tied to me. But do you think it's any different for shifters? I can't stop my wolf from craving you. I can't stop myself from wanting to protect you and doing anything to ensure that. *I* don't have a *choice*. Jesus, Kalinda. If I did, this may seem like something impossible, but I'd *still* want you."

Exactly how was she supposed to answer that? Most of the last few months had been nothing but a whirlwind of random burps of her magic flaring in ways she didn't understand, the Chaos Realm, the Council—oh, and the death sentence—and now she was mated.

But … *choose* her? He didn't *know* her.

Why was everyone trying to change her life and make her feel bad about it? Nobody would deal with all of this without breaking, and she was barely keeping it together. She just wanted … a moment to think, to get her head clear. Anything but to keep fighting.

She took a deep breath. *Kalinda, sort through it.* She heard her grandmother's voice as clear as if she were sitting right next to her. She'd always said a woman was defined by how she dealt with the curveballs in her life. So what was Kalinda really feeling? That was the question.

Romano was gorgeous, and not in a superficial way, but he'd handled her lashing out, fighting him every step of the way, and still stood beside her. She didn't doubt his entire pack was putting themselves on the line to do for her what they were doing. And she couldn't forget what Romano and Dominic did.

At the end of the day, the Lombardi Pack was full of Made Wolves who lived by a code of violence and power. It wasn't just their wolves that made them dominating and always moving forward. They lived to lead and control their interests with an iron fist. Romano was dealing with her situation the same way. She'd seen how Dominic had done the same with Zoey.

But Kalinda had always prided herself on caring for her own matters, running her business, and protecting her girls. She kept her head down, built her empire slowly, and tried to live as human-like as possible in a place where magic lived and breathed.

And now …

"It's too much, Romano."

For the first time in forever, she took a leap. She was afraid of it all. Of how this would completely change her life.

"I never really talk about it, but I was going to get married."

Romano growled, and she rolled her eyes. "Pipe down, Fido. I loved him. I had a plan to own my restaurant and live as his wife. To have my family around me, the white picket fence. And then the FBMC scanned my hometown. I never thought of it, of having mage blood. I couldn't do anything but make good food, but they told me I needed to move to a portal city. I thought …" she swallowed.

Dammit, it still hurt. After all this time.

"I thought he'd come with me, that he loved me enough to follow through with our dreams, but he walked away instead. I was tainted. So I lost my family and my fiancé. I lost everything, and I never had a say. Some freaking organization told me what my new life was going to be and I scraped until I rebuilt the pieces."

Romano sat on the bed, close enough she could feel his heat. His gaze locked on hers. As much as she hated to admit it, he was a rock in the storm. He was so strong. His broad shoulders were barely contained in his black button-up. His hands rested in his lap, large and capable of both a deadly action and a caring touch. She could see the hammer of his gun as it rested in an underarm holster. This man was here, with her, watching over her as she slept. Protecting her when she was at her weakest. This man had claimed her and took it all with a crooked smile.

But that smile was gone now. All that remained was a man looking at a woman, listening, and all the joviality of his normal self was wiped away. She felt like she was seeing him for the first time—the man beneath the mask.

"You aren't broken, Kalinda. And he was a piece of shit for not fighting for what belonged to him. He should have told you, no matter what, you were enough for him. You were worth it."

He lifted one hand and traced the bite on her neck with a callused fingertip. "This mark means you are my enough. That's all. That on a bad day, I choose you. On days the world requires too much, you can give me the burden. And when you're in danger, I'm the shield. It means you are never going to be alone again. I'm so sorry you've been alone for so long."

How did he know? How did he understand? The loneliness had eaten at her, twisted her until she couldn't trust anyone to get too close.

"Everyone leaves, Romano."

He sighed, cupping the back of her neck. Heat slid down her spine, pulling her nipples taut as she sucked in a tight breath.

"My mother didn't want my father. She hated being mated to him. Craved to be free. She never understood why her wolf bowed to him and let him claim her, and she never let he or I forget it. By the time she disappeared, I'd learned mating didn't always mean forever, and those closet to you can rip out your heart."

She hadn't known.

Kalinda opened her mouth to speak, but he shook his head. "I don't want to repeat the same mistakes my mother did. I won't hold a woman to me who doesn't want to be here. But I also won't let you run away. You're better than that."

He pulled her into his body until they were chest to chest, their mouths a breath apart. "My woman fights. She claws, bites, and commands until she gets just what she wants. But she does not run. She may bend, she may even break, but she's strong enough to pick up every fucking piece and put it back together. My woman is strong enough to claim just what she wants."

Every word slipped into her soul. Heated breath skittered across her sensitive skin. She'd never been intimate like this, their eyes on each other, touching in a way like sex and yet so still. Her pulse jumped in her neck, and his fingers reflexively caressed the spot. Each time she exhaled, he inhaled.

"I can't seem to do that right now," she admitted.

Romano smiled, a brilliant white grin full of sharp teeth and wicked promise. "Oh, but you can and you will. I'm here to block anything and everyone from taking away the time you need to do just that."

His fingers clenched around her neck, and she gripped the front of his shirt. "I don't know how to do this."

Fuck me running.

His tongue traced her full lower lip. A taunt. A challenge. That same odd feeling tightened her chest. Her magic. She stiffened, afraid of the heat slipping from her. Her blood was sluggish, too thick in her veins.

"Romano," she warned.

He never let her go. His grip was an anchor, strong and sure. Ribbons of gold and black slid across her vision. *It is in color just like Silva said.* She'd never seen it before, but her magic reached for Romano. It wrapped around his arms, and his nostrils flared. Still, he didn't move.

"No matter what it does, I'm still going to wait on you."

Wait on her? What was he talking about? But the questions whipped out of her head too quickly for her to answer. She was too hot. Too tense. Too *everything*.

"Don't let it take you. What are you feeling?"

Need. Desire. *Craving.*

God, every time her magic flared when he was around, she wanted to jump on him like an alley cat. What the hell was wrong with her? But then, it also did the same to others when it got out of control around them.

What the hell?

He jerked her by her neck, a quick shake hard enough to snatch her out of her thoughts. "What are you feeling?" he repeated.

"Need."

"For?"

You. Kalinda almost said it, but she bit her lip. It was a freaking study in solar flares between her legs. She'd never felt her heartbeat there, pulsing and throbbing. She was slick, achy. Romano's nostrils flared again.

"Every time," he forced out past a growl.

"What?"

He shook his head. "You're going to say it. You have to figure it out."

Her power. What it was doing. She hated to admit it, but he was trying to help her. But she was too frustrated to—dammit.

"Sex," she mumbled.

"I can't hear you."

Damn wolf could hear everything. But she still threw her shoulders back, daring him to laugh at her. "Sex."

"Every time?"

"Yes."

"And?"

He wasn't going to let it go. He wanted everything, demanded her to face it. Demanded her to be the woman she could be. She took a deep breath, taking in his masculine scent. "Sex … with you."

His grin could only be described as wolfish.

"So you wanted me to eat you."

God, that shouldn't have made her clench. But it did.

"I can't do this, Romano. I can't do mindless. I can't do freefall."

"Why not? I'm going to be there to catch you."

"And after? You can't think I'm going to believe in forever."

Once more, his smile disappeared and she got the real Romano. "You don't have to believe in forever. Believe in the fight. I won't give up … and neither will you."

He crashed his mouth into hers, and on some silent accord, they still kept their gazes locked. Other than his hands on the back of her neck, their lips were all that touched. Romano claimed her, forcing her mouth open with his tongue and tasting his way over every surface inside. Slick, silken lips slid against hers with precision, fitting them together. He turned her head slightly, deepening the kiss.

She'd never been touched like this. With his mouth alone he proved she'd been missing more than she'd ever known. How did one be claimed with sensuous power? He sucked her tongue into his mouth and bit it, testing the firmness against his teeth, and it sent her desire through the roof. She wanted to feel his teeth on her skin, on her breasts, along her rib cage, between her legs, *everywhere*.

That dance against a razor-sharp edge.

Kalinda knew he was strong enough to physically break her, rip her to shreds, and something in that strength made her weep with need. No one had ever been strong enough. She' always had to temper her fire, her rage, her emotions, her words. Every step had to be careful controlled and managed. Head up, shoulders back, walk strong, run her business, maintain her image. She'd never truly let her hair down. But he forced her, ripping any command she thought she had right out of her hands.

Finally, he plunged his fingers into her hair, scattering her carefully placed bobby pins and gripping the strands. Each prick of near pain reminded her of his overwhelming power against hers. She sank into him, letting him lead.

It feels good to let go.

To give in.

To be cared for.

His hand placement allowed for his arms to cage her against his chest and take her weight. She didn't run away. Instead, she gave him more. Pushing into him, she craved more. Kalinda didn't realize he was moving them until her legs straightened.

Her feet didn't touch the floor.

He held her with the strength of his arms, hovering off the floor. *That's hot.*

He broke their kiss. "You're wearing too many clothes. How much do you like of what you have on?"

She blinked. "Clothes?"

He chuckled. "Good answer. Grip the poster rail above your head."

Romano maneuvered until one arm was wrapped around her waist so she could reach up and grip the iron rail above his bed.

"You're so beautiful."

She could see just enough in the darkened room as he lifted his free hand and partially shifted until he had sharp claws.

"Don't move," he ordered.

His claws raked through her top, bra, pants, and underwear like warm butter, leaving her exposed, her breasts full and plump, nipples hard, and her trimmed curls damp. He cupped her hot center, his sharp nails resting against the base.

Danger. Edge.

"Trust me."

Romano lowered slowly, taking her weight on his shoulders, and kissed down her neck. His teeth grazed across her heated skin. Collar bone. Sternum. Over the swell of her right breast before his tongue snaked out and laved one nipple. He kept going, starting fires and setting them to smolder with his damn kisses and sharp bites.

He'd read her mind, he had to. He bit and kissed his way down every spot she'd wanted him to. Touched each place she'd needed until she was panting. He knelt between her legs, her thighs on either side of his head.

When he looked up at her, his eyes flashed golden for a moment.

"Every bit of power you have pent up, waiting to rush out, I want you to give to me. Don't hold it, don't think about it. Let this be the safe place."

"Romano," she started.

He bit her inner left thigh, hard.

I like that.

"I'm not asking, Kalinda."

She closed her eyes. Could she? What if—

His hot tongue licked over her curls and down, swirling around her clit without touching it. Her body tensed, muscles locked in anticipation. Magic jerked in her chest, demanding release. She gasped, nearly choked with it.

One deep breath. *In. Out.*

And then she let go.

Of all of it.

CHAPTER *ELEVEN*

Romano's silken tongue was the counterbalance to Kalinda's complete loss of control. Magic, alive and breathing, crested within her blood and, for the first time, was freed of all inhibitions and controls. Like a second lover, it caressed her skin, heated her blood, and ignited her senses. Sex was heavy in the air—a combination of her sweetness and Romano's rugged, earthy scent. Her gifts swirled in her mouth, leaving behind traces of chocolate and spice even as Romano sucked her clit into his mouth and flicked it eagerly with his tongue.

He applied hot, steady pressure on the nub, giving her no escape and even less room to understand the sensations pouring through her. A heartbeat thundered in her ears, deeper and heavier than her own. Scalding breath danced over her heated flesh, sending shockwaves reverberating through her. His fingers were harsh, digging into her hips, and she had no doubt she'd be bruised in the morning.

Then … it changed.

A lone wolfed howled deep inside her mind, exhilarated with happiness. It raced through the forest, large paws well-balanced on deep, moist earth, each scent a signal to the world around it. And it was free. So free. Explosive with its craving for what danced right before it. Silken walls, taut skin, slick juices sliding along its tongue.

Mate.

Kalinda sucked in a deep breath, as did the wolf, filling both their lungs with a heady call of the wild. And the wolf answered, reveling in want and desire and wrapped in musky notes of a perfect red wine. Shivers raced along the wolf's spine, and with sudden clarity, she knew the wolf was Romano, the flavor *her*.

Somehow, her pleasure, spiraling up from her belly and wringing cries from her throat with every bated breath, mixed with his—his love of feeling her folds, the craving of her taste, the blossoming of overwhelming need.

They were one and separate, together and not, racing toward climax. She'd never had anyone in her life she could think of who truly wanted her the way he did. Romano's need of her made her toes curl and her back arch. It only served to make the electricity arcing through her body as tight as a bow string, ready to snap at any moment.

A growl vibrated against the inside of her thighs and slid deep into her core. Romano used the flat of his tongue to trace a molten path from the base of her up to her mound and back down again.

"I could eat you all night, Kalinda. Devour you like my last meal."

Yeah, her fingers slipped from the railing above her head right about then. Her back bowed. Romano pressed his face back into her mound and tossed her into the stratosphere even as he lowered her to the bed. The soft mattress and comforter cushioned her, enveloping her in feather lightness.

Trapped between Romano and the bed, Kalinda rode the wave. She couldn't stop her scream if she tried. Couldn't hold back from clenching her thighs around his ears and burying her fingers in the cool thickness of his hair. She gripped the strands, yanking him harder against her, curling her lower body and riding his face.

It was magnetic.

It was wild.

It was like nothing she'd ever experienced before.

By the time she slumped back and away, she could barely catch her breath. Romano stood, casting a deep shadow across her and the bed. His silhouette cut a striking figure as he removed his holster. The heavy thud of the gun was loud against as it hit the nightstand. His motions were meticulous and slow.

Agonizingly slow.

She was afraid he would ruin the tempo and send her sliding down back into awareness, but as she watched him, anticipation grew. His shoulders were powerful, uncaged from the confines of his shirt, and his waist tapered into a pronounced V of muscle. She traced the indentions with her gaze as his hands worked on his belt.

Romano was a man chiseled and built for war. Scarring marred his chest, something she'd never seen on a wolf. Kalinda reached out before she realized it, sitting up slightly to touch the puckered flesh.

"We've both had our time in the Chaos Realm."

His words were deep, his gaze heavy with remembered pain. Later, she'd ask, but for now, she only wanted this moment between them.

Letting her hands trail down the hard build of his stomach, she smiled saucily. "My warrior."

He froze, fire blazing in his gaze for a moment before he ripped his clothes from his body and pushed her back onto the bed. He was heavy, making it hard for her chest to fully expand, but his weight was welcome. Rough hands gripped her thighs and pushed them up and out until she had to plant her feet on the bed for balance. Then, the smooth head of his cock slid against her folds.

"There is no turning back now."

He didn't give her a chance to respond. He gripped her throat, a warning, a promise, pressing against her pulse and constricting her airflow enough to make her head spin. His other hand braced her hips where he wanted them before he slammed home.

Kalinda choked out a cry, his girth stretching her to burning, his length filling her, and the crisp edge of pain was nearly too much. Gripping the wrists of the hand holding her throat, she dug her nails into his skin.

A metallic tang rent the air, but Romano's jackknifing hips didn't stop. They clashed together, nothing soft or subtle about it. She'd called him a warrior, and her body became a battlefield he was intent on conquering. He kept her pinned down with his hand, but his free one roamed her curves. Each place he passed scorched her nerve endings and made her womb clench.

He tweaked her nipples, and she groaned. He molded her breasts so he could sip at their curves, and she sighed. When he fingered her clit, she screamed. He left nowhere untouched, turning her skin into a livewire. Her magic still filled the room, gold and black touching every crevice and pressing against the walls.

"Fuck, I need more." Romano jerked out of her and flipped her over.

Too tired to do anything more than follow his lead, Kalinda let him position her on her hands and knees. His heat burned her as he draped over her, his mouth hot against her shoulder. He wrapped his arm around her, forearm pressed between her breasts and fingers finding that familiar place around her neck. Using his free hand, he pulled her back onto his cock.

They met in the center, and now his possession was deeper, more profound. Gone was the rough pounding, replaced by deep thrusts.

His teeth slid into her neck, right where he'd marked her.

Fuck the sun; she knew something much hotter—Romano.

Kalinda didn't know where she ended and he began. Whether they had two heartbeats or one. Everything twisted and turned, combined and slid into place until they were pieces of the same picture. Her mouth hung open, and soundless screams were all she could manage. It was too much and not enough. Each caress of his shaft within her played notes of possession and craving. She followed, unable to do much more, too lost in her own slip of control. She let Romano lead the charge. By the time he roared his release, she didn't even know her own name.

"Well, you do get messy every once in a while."

Whoever had interrupted Kalinda's much-needed sleep was going to get a pointy stiletto right in the center of their forehead. Even if she felt like all she did was sleep lately, thanks to her shiny new sex magic … or was it that *she* was just horny? Whatever. Last night's sleep was much different. Romano hadn't left her alone until the sun rose, and according to her eyes' stubborn refusal to open, she'd bet she'd been asleep for a few hours at best.

"Come on, woman."

Oh, yum. Even her sleepy mind would recognize the stimulating aroma of a robust coffee with Irish butter. And only one other person—besides maybe Zoey, who wouldn't dare wake her up like this—knew she drank her coffee like that. Kalinda opened one eye to find Silva leaning over one side of the bed, a large steaming cup of joe in her petite hand. Of course, she didn't look like herself at all.

"What the hell?"

Silva arched a brow but didn't comment. Okay, it was completely weird to see Silva in a skintight, long-sleeve black getup with sterling silver plates across her breasts and abdomen. And was that a *hilt* over her shoulder?

There was not enough coffee in the world for this.

Kalinda sat up, making sure to tuck the cover around her naked form—this was so inappropriate for a boss to employee relationship—and grasped the offered coffee. Ten minutes and one cup down, Kalinda stuck out the cup for a refill. Silva, bless her, just smiled and disappeared.

Kalinda jumped out of bed to get dressed, but her wobbly legs and sticky thighs reminded her of how much fun she'd had last night.

Yeah, not going to think about the mating part, or how good it felt, or how close we came, or even the emotions leaking through our weird, magic sexytime thing.

She raced into the bathroom, slamming the door just as Silva came back into the room.

"I'll leave gear on the bed and coffee on the nightstand. Put your hair up in the bun you like so much and I'll meet you in the living room. You've got twenty minutes."

Kalinda frowned at the bathroom door. "Who died and made *you* boss?"

"Things change, Ales."

Wait, how did Silva know about that? Driven to know exactly what was going on, and wondering where Romano was anyway, she raced through her morning ritual. She came out of the bathroom— that was completely going to get a long appointment with her in the future because *whoa*—and found a similar black and silver outfit waiting for her.

Once she had it on—figuring out the mage-elastic allowed her to pull it up over her body and it formed to her shape—she had to admit it was stunning as she admired it in the bathroom mirror. Her dark hair pulled into a bun made her angular cheekbones stand out, and her shape was accented. She looked alluring and deadly at the same time. That was a first.

Kalinda grabbed her second cup of coffee and guzzled it down on the way to the living room. Silva was there waiting, sipping her own cup of coffee.

She let out a low whistle. "I'm happy Romano isn't here. He would never let you outside in that."

"Romano doesn't tell me what to do."

Silva snorted. "Says the newly mated woman. Right."

"Silva, I know we've been working well together, but this is a bit weird. I followed the instructions, but now I need clarity. Why are you here? And how do you know about the Ales?"

Silva put her cup down and placed her hands in her lap. "Romano called me. He had to go to a meeting with the Moretti and Lombardi Pack powers that be, and when he told me what happened with you, I knew I needed to be here."

Well, that answered the questions of where Romano was. Though she would have liked to get some sort of message or something. *Ugh, it was already starting.* That's why she didn't do stuff like this. Trust was hard earned, and most men wouldn't be able to keep up with her demands. She'd always known this.

"He left you a note on the bed, but I moved it in here when I woke you. Wasn't sure if you were going to smack the coffee out of my hand or not."

Sure as shit, Silva held a white note with black scrawl in her hand.

Headed to a meeting but made sure you have protection. If you need me, I'm now speed dial one on your phone.
Sorry,
Zoey.

She couldn't help but smile. Zoey would lose her shit, of course, but Kalinda would make sure she was number two. Silva chuckled, and Kalinda cleared her throat, embarrassed to be caught grinning like some teenager in a new relationship.

"Okay, but that doesn't explain it all," Kalinda told her.

"You know I'm Fae? There are blood pacts for Fae kin to be attached to certain families. The agreements are as old as time and can't be broken. The minute I knew you were an Ales, it made sense why I've been so drawn to you."

"The thing you couldn't tell me before was that you were drawn to me," Kalinda figured. "It might have been a bit weird to tell an employer you were applying for the job because their blood called."

"A bit. Although, I didn't know that's what it was. I just couldn't stay away."

"You just left home?"

Silva frowned. "I don't know."

"You don't know?"

"I can't remember. When I told you there were things I couldn't tell you, I meant it. Most of my memory is a fog, and when I try too hard to remember, it hurts."

"Hurts?" Kalinda felt like a parrot. *Polly, want a cracker?*

"Yes. It's hard to describe, but everything inside of me wants to shrivel up and die. So since I like living, I don't try so hard anymore."

"I'm sorry, Silva."

Silva shrugged. "I make do. What I can say is I figured why your magic worked on me in your kitchen the other day when it didn't the first time."

That got Kalinda's attention. With the Viscount Pride Debacle—naming things was cool—Silva had been aware the entire time. She'd gotten the girls out of there before making sure she could tell Dominic and Romano what had happened when they showed up. Kalinda had wondered why Silva was so messed up the second time. At least she could finally get some answers.

"Why?"

"Because I ate it."

Did the sun just come into the room?

Just hearing the word "ate" made her pulse jump and her thighs clench. Jesus, but she'd be a full course meal for Romano any day. How the hell she'd never taken him up on that offer before was pure sacrilege. Maybe she'd add some toppings next time—

"Earth to Kalinda."

Dammit! Kalinda slicked her hair and regained her composure. "Continue."

"You know, wolves have pretty long tongues."

"Continue, Silva!"

"Fine, fine. You're so much fun; I never knew. Anyway, when I ate your food infused with your magic, it was able to get past my natural defenses to magic."

An idea formed in Kalinda's mind. "Does that mean you're immune to the Council? That could solve a lot of problems."

"Unfortunately, no. They're strong enough to direct their gifts at me. Fae blood may give me an edge, like shifters, but we agreed to give up some of our strength against magic when we joined the FBMC."

The faraway look in Silva's gaze made Kalinda stay quiet, unsure if Silva even realized she was sharing knowledge. Kalinda was afraid if she pointed it out, Silva would feel pain at remembering.

"Once we joined, we—" She stopped suddenly and gripped her stomach with a moan.

Kalinda rushed forward. "Don't try to remember anymore. It's okay. We'll figure it out."

After a few breaths, Silva nodded. "I'm sorry."

"Don't apologize. At least we know you can be affected by my magic if I feed you, so maybe you just can't have any of my delicious food. Too bad for you."

"I'm not so sure."

"Why?"

"Because it smells different now. More contained."

That gave Kalinda pause. She'd been having problems controlling her magic for some time. Hearing that it may be within better control was pretty awesome. But the only thing that had changed was … sex. Seriously?

"You're lying."

"Not even a little bit. Maybe playing Little Red with the Big Bad Wolf gave you some practice."

"It can't be that easy."

"Or maybe it is, to a point. Magic can be demanding. You can't ignore it. When it wants you, it will have you. Denying it only makes it push stronger. If you accepted it, then it could be more subtle in you now."

Kalinda rolled her eyes. "Sleeping with him did not fix me."

"Oh, but maybe it did. Let's test it. Shoot some my way."

"I'd rather not."

"That's the point of the armor we have on. It's Fae-built and cost more than a pixie whore on premium night, but Romano didn't blink. He wants you safe and working with a Fae who can handle it. Besides …" Silva leaned over the counter to grab a knife. She hefted the weight of the handle a minute before tossing it lightning fast through the air. It embedded in the opposite wall with a *thwack*. "I have other skills too that might be useful for you to use."

"Where the hell did you learn that?"

"I'm sort of tired of saying 'I don't know,' so let's just leave it at I can fight. You need to learn to do the same. Romano thought you'd like having a way to defend yourself instead of always relying on others."

Romano was there every step of the way. Through her fight, through her fear, through denying him, he constantly showed how he thought of her and was willing to make this work. Kalinda may not be completely with this mated thing and doing something crazy like falling in love, but she couldn't deny it felt nice to have someone on her side like that.

Damn, Houston, we may have a problem.

CHAPTER *TWELVE*

Romano never really thought about having a mate. At least, not past the idea his wolf might choose one and he'd have to face it. Most of the time, he enjoyed life and women in a superficial capacity; he was too caught up with working for the Family.

Before becoming a *Capo* under Dominic, he'd been an Enforcer under Dominic for Arturo. That meant death and violence, blood and order, without much room for softness. And while they'd made some changes to the organization, they were still, at the core, dangerous men living dangerous lives. Now he had a mate, and he had to think of her safety as well as his. It was unfamiliar territory.

The thought overwhelmed him as he walked into the Arena to meet with Arturo and his men about the Viscount Pride. Dominic walked beside him, eyes forward and silent, a partner in this movement to keep their women safe. Part of Romano wanted to return to their bed, take her many more times, and enjoy days of learning every cry, every inch of her, and the multitude of ways he could make her climax. Even with all that, the urge to keep her alive was paramount.

There was a great chance, one he feared, of her turning wolf and facing great pain when she did. He didn't know much about

Born Wolves turning their mates who were high-level mages, but it seemed the success rate was high; however, there was no telling what would happen at the combination. The mating of a Born Wolf with a mage over Level 6 hadn't been done before.

Not only that, the Council would come for her eventually, though they would have to plan their move to keep from inciting a war. The Viscount Pride had their hand in this, and there was also no telling how they would be able to get out from under the Council's death sentence if she decided against going with their wishes. There were too many dangers, too many unknowns, and it made Romano's wolf uncomfortable.

"Quiet on you makes me nervous." Finally breaking the silence, Dominic was sharp as they stopped in the middle of packed earth dyed red from the blood of contenders. They stood in one of the few places wolves could fight to the death in fighting for bets and glory. Even some disputes could be settled within these hallowed walls where the air smelled like death.

It had been years, of course, since anyone was willing to challenge Dominic or Romano. "There are too many factors. I can't just run in and kill everyone like I'd normally do."

"It's tempting. I know the feeling. Did you settle things with Kalinda?"

Romano sighed. "As much as we can. A breakthrough with that woman one day could be just a crack in the armor the next."

"So you called for backup."

"Hey, Silva is going to train Kalinda when I can't be there. I call that a smart business move."

Dominic started walking with a snort, and Romano fell into step with him. "You're chicken shit, that's what happened. Admit it."

"I don't understand those words. Did you say you're a baby douche?"

"Why a baby douche instead of just a douche?"

"Sounds like you just called yourself a double baby douche, and that's really sad. They probably have support groups for that."

Dominic's laughter trailed with them as they got into the lone elevator off the main floor and pressed the lower of only two buttons. The doors slid closed and they descended. "At least your sense of humor is still intact."

"Always. I should probably go on the road."

"I'd buy all your tickets and not show up just so you can have an empty stadium."

"But did I make money off your sale though? I'd win."

Dominic shook his head before all levity left his face when the elevator doors slid open. Here, when the meeting of the bosses commenced, there were no openings for laughter. Within these walls they decided on life or death.

Arturo was already seated to one side of the table, Carlo at his right hand. Carlo had taken Dominic's place at Arturo's side after he had dispatched Primo and Ottavio to the underworld.

Carlo acknowledged them first, inclining his head to Dominic. "You've made it."

As Dominic reached his chair, he greeted Arturo. "What have you found out?"

"The Viscount Pride was hired by the Council to cause a situation in which Kalinda would be taken under their custody and then handed over to the Council," Arturo answered.

"What would that earn them?"

"I figured you would ask that, so I wanted us all to hear it."

Doors to the right opened up and two Enforcers, faces hard, dragged in a blond man, blood caked into the golden strands of his hair and down the side of his face, into the room. He was shirtless, and his pants were barely hanging on. His flesh was a tapestry of cuts and bruises. Not that Romano gave a shit at all. That fucking pride had targeted his mate, and he wanted to know why.

"This is Bastion, the Leo of Viscount Pride's brother," Arturo explained.

Romano whistled. Arturo was never kind when he wanted information. Snatching Orion's brother sent a message Kalinda was not to be touched.

"What did your brother get from selling out to the Council?"

Bastion spat on the ground. "Didn't one of yours join Benedict? Who's the sellout?"

One of the Enforcers raised a meaty fist and all of Bastion's bravado leaked out of him in one sharp whimper.

"I won't ask again," Dominic warned.

"Mating rights and your land."

Dominic stood, pulling his gun from his side. Bastion's eyes widened until the whites were prominent, and he tried to put his hands in front of his face. The Enforcer's hold on him prevented him from completing the action.

"Please," he begged.

Just a mere step away, Dominic stopped and let his gun rest at his side. "My lands? If you joined the Council, they promised you mating rights to *whom?*"

Bastion swallowed. "We'd claim the mage, Kalinda, and the earth witch, Zoey."

Romano was on his feet the instant Kalinda's name was mentioned. Too fast for the eye to follow, Dominic lifted his gun and fired, blasting a hole in Bastion's leg. Bastion jerked in shock and let out a scream of pain.

"Shift," Dominic ordered, using his Alpha power. The air crackled, but Romano was so furious he barely felt the sharp little sparks. Bastion wailed but turned instantly, his lion springing free, snarling and sharp, black claws exposed. He crouched, ready to leap, but Dominic stopped him.

"Shift."

Bastion's scream filled the room. Shifting from lion to human had healed most of his injuries and the bullet wound was closed, pink flesh puckering. A longer stay in his lion form would heal it entirely, but Dominic was hot with rage and it made him cruel. He'd forced the lion to shift fast enough to heal the wound but hadn't given his body a chance to push out the bullet. The residual pain from a forced shifting would be killer too.

Romano didn't care about that either. Before he even thought about it, he pulled his gun and shot Bastion in the other leg. Dominic never missed a beat, forcing Bastion to shift from man to lion and back again.

"Those women are mated," Arturo added, his voice deceptively lazy. "And one of them carries the heir of both the Moretti and Lombardi Packs."

Bastion stuttered for a moment. "We weren't told that. Only that doing this would elevate our place with the Council, and we'd be given high-level mages to give extra power to our bloodline."

"Which one?" Romano wasn't sure why he wanted to know, but he did. "Which one had you and your brother chosen?"

Bastion refused to answer, so Romano lifted his gun again. Bastion's answer came out in a rush. "I was going to get the earth witch and my brother the other."

Arturo shifted in his seat. "So the Council put you on Kalinda's trail to capture her?"

"The one with the shop? Yes. We were to monitor her. My brother once passed by her shop while she and the other woman were in there. Her wards on the shop reacted to a vampire, but her scent still came through. We'd been told to smell for old magic. Once we did, it was reported to the Council and plans were made to take her."

It didn't make sense. Why would the Council go through all that trouble when they could have quietly taken her themselves? Benedict's betrayal hadn't become obvious by then, so how would they have even known in the first place? There were always more fucking questions than answers.

"What tipped the Council's hand about her?"

"They didn't tell us. We just had a job to do and take the girl so the Council would give us what we wanted. The wolves have ruled long enough. It's our turn."

"You say it in present tense like it's going to happen," Romano forced out through gritted teeth.

Bastion's eyes glowed with anger. "My brother will never stop," he sneered, still arrogant and clueless.

"Well, let's send him a message to encourage him to make better choices, shall we?" Arturo's words rolled out on a slow, deadly growl.

Arturo nodded, and the Enforcers lifted Bastion off his feet. Bastion's eyes went wide with fear; he knew what that meant. He thrashed and bucked against them, his fangs thrusting from his gums, but their grip on him was like iron.

"Make sure his brother gets *all* the messages."

Piece by piece.

Bastion kicked and snarled and tried to shift yet again, yellow fur flowing over his face. Dominic sent out another wave of Alpha power and forced him back into his human form, wrenching a shriek of pain from the panicked animal.

The wolves watched as the screeching, struggling lion was hauled from the room.

It wasn't something they did often, but the Leo of Viscount Pride had moved to claim two mated women. Kalinda may not have been mated when they'd been put on her trail, but Zoey had been, and there was no way they hadn't known. Even Kalinda's Katering would have been run over with the scent of wolves, a warning to anyone wanting to encroach. Not a single one of them sitting at the table was going to ignore such a violation without violence.

"I'm surprised you didn't have him think of a number between one and two hundred like we used to do," Carlo commented.

"I find myself getting a little lenient in my older age," Arturo returned.

Carlo snorted. "Yeah, so lenient you'll be sending him to his brother in pieces."

"It absolutely is. I could have kept him alive while the pieces were made."

To punctuate his thoughts, a single gunshot rang out loudly, echoing through the room.

"At least we know why the Viscount Pride was willing to challenge us to get Kalinda out of there. What the Council orchestrated in dangerous. Yes, Kalinda is my mate, but maneuvering whole power structures in Encantado?"

"They never would have given the Viscount Pride half of what they promised. It would have been impossible, and the pride was just too stupid and greedy to see that. But we don't know if everyone on the Council was privy to those plans or not," Arturo argued.

"I have no doubt Lennox was in on it. He wants Kalinda."

Romano remembered how the bastard had touched her like she belonged to him or was meant for him. He still planned on killing the bastard at a later date.

"It doesn't matter right now," Carlo offered. "We know what the pride's game was, and we can keep protection at a heightened level. The Leo will want to retaliate, but the message may be enough to remind him he is pushing things far above his strength. All we need to do is protect the women and wait to see what happens when the time is up for Kalinda's shifting."

"We still don't know how to get her out of the death sentence," Romano argued. "Kalinda isn't going to accept joining the Council after the way they've done her, and we still face that. Joining the

Council would mean she'd be locked to their lands and under their control. It won't matter that I am her mate. They may have to allow me access to her or confine me to living beside her."

"Neither of which is an option," Dominic promised. "Zahara is the only high-level mage who was able to turn down the Council and survive."

"You won't be able to follow Zahara's path," Arturo warned.

"Why?" Romano had never seen Arturo look as deadly as he did at that moment.

Dominic tensed. He hadn't relaxed since Bastion's exposure of the Viscount Pride's play in all of this. But he was rock solid now.

For moment, surprise broke through before the shutters came back down over Arturo's face. "We will discuss it later."

"I am not one of your wolves any longer, Arturo," Dominic argued.

Threat and domination whipped through the room. Romano maneuvered to be behind his Alpha, even as Carlo did the same with Arturo. The two pairs faced off in the center of the room, one Alpha against another, their Enforcers at their side.

Not exactly how this meeting was supposed to go.

"You think you have what it takes to go after me, pup?"

"We can sure as fuck see how it goes."

And that was not going to help.

Romano grimaced, knowing what he was about to do could get his head ripped off, but so be it. There were much more important things going on than an Alpha pissing contest. Dominic would just have to hate him now and thank him later.

He stepped in front of his Alpha, and domination and control immediately washed over him. The tight, puckered skin of scarring on his face itched. He gritted his teeth, trying against everything to stay on his damn feet with a ton of bricks weighing down on his shoulders. *Submit. Submit. Alpha.* His wolf was snarling and biting, warring against the human side of Romano. His wolf didn't understand what he was doing, only that he should never stand up against his Alpha.

Chill the fuck out, man. I'm trying to stop a bloodbath here.

Of course, that was much harder when he was down on one knee between two of the most powerful men in Encantado. It was hard enough just to catch his breath. But he held firm, forcing his gaze to meet Dominic's and keeping his head straight instead of exposing the soft area of his neck.

Romano's voice was a barely contained snarl. "I'm all for power play, but normally I'm on top, so could you calm down long enough to see this epic shit here? Only happens once in a lifetime."

Dominic's gaze flashed, his pupils dilating and filling up most of the iris around them. His wolf was close to the surface. "Move, Romano."

Another blast of power made Romano's insides twist viciously. *That's going to hurt in the morning.* "Zoey."

One second. Two. Nothing changed, and yet everything did. Dominic's shoulders relaxed a fraction, and his jaw wasn't so tight, the muscle working double time instead of triple.

"Zoey," Dominic repeated.

"Yeah, and she's in danger. Maybe we should focus on that?"

Dominic glared at Arturo as he put a hand on Romano's shoulder and released his power on him. Romano breathed a deep sigh of relief.

"We'll discuss this later," Dominic promised.

"Yes, I'm sure we will. We won't have a choice. But all the players aren't here for that one, and I want you focused where you need to be," Arturo answered.

"I'm not your concern any longer, Arturo. I have my own pack now."

For the first time, Arturo looked ... soft. As soft as rock can appear smoothed over by years of wear and tear. Romano got to his feet stiffly, joints cracking as he realigned. He never wanted to face challenging the Alpha power again. But everyone had eyes on Arturo, and Carlo even went as far as to step closer to Arturo.

"You have always been my concern, Dom. It was not always just because you were a wolf of my pack or my right hand." He paused. "You know I had a family once, yes?"

Dominic nodded slowly. "Yes."

No one said the rest: they were murdered and who murdered them was never found. To speak of Arturo's family meant death, and he didn't often bring it up himself. When he did, it was during quiet moments with Dominic in attendance and Romano at his side. Romano kept silent, knowing this.

"Then trust me when I say, we will speak on this later, Dominic. This is the one time I am speaking as a father instead of an Alpha. My men are already on their way to your lands for added protection. We have less than a month to figure out a way to say no to the Trinity or prepare for war with them. Let us focus on that."

Dominic only nodded, and Romano couldn't blame him. What exactly could you say to a man who always chose derisive and violent action instead of sentiment but had chosen to show emotion and care in this instance? Romano and his Alpha remained silent until they got into the elevator to leave.

"Well, that was just fucking weird," Romano commented.

"You couldn't last three minutes without saying something, could you?"

"What? It was awkward, and I don't *do* awkward. It makes my balls shrivel."

"I hate you. I really do."

"Yeah? Love you too, douche."

"How shriveled are your balls after saying that?"

"Microscopic. Want to see?"

"Why in the shit ... you know what? Never mind. Let's just get home."

What else could they do?

CHAPTER *THIRTEEN*

"**Y**ou have to visualize what you're wanting to happen, Kalinda, or it won't work."

It had been a week of *hell*. Kicks, flips, muscle straining, a whole lot of sweating, and mental exercises. Silva was a damn workaholic, and since the moment she'd been put on "whip Kalinda into shape" duty, she'd been a tyrant.

"Kalinda!"

"If you say my name one more time, I'm going to send you to the floor screaming. I swear."

Silva, the minx, only smiled before sticking out her tongue. "You can try."

Challenge accepted.

Kalinda practiced what Silva had showed her: picturing her magic in her mind. She associated colors with the skill. Red for anger, blue for calm, purple for manipulation, white for force, black for fear, and … well, the gold *really* liked Romano and caused orgies, so she figured that was all about sex.

"Totally not focusing," Silva teased.

Kalinda's face grew hot. *Whatever*. She focused on Silva and pulled her magic close, swirling it from the air. She didn't know why she chose to view it that way, or use it like that, but it seemed to work for her. Each time she attempted to do it with traditional methods, it sputtered and flickered out, but literally pulling it out of thin air worked best.

Sort of. Everybody feels these things, right? Must be residuals just hanging out here.

The more she focused, the more a purple haze appeared around Silva. That was new too, as she'd learned better control with her magic. Kalinda couldn't make it happen instantly just yet, but she could see her magic with the naked eye.

Silva wasn't smiling now.

"Okay, turn off the twisting-my-insides thing."

"What's that? I don't hear any screaming."

Not that she *really* wanted to make Silva hurt that much, but her word was her word.

Romano came into the clearing, Zoey trailing behind him. "The roses, Zoey. We're growing *roses* not daffodils."

Zoey scoffed. "And what's wrong with daffodils?"

"They're pansies, that's what. The roses had thorns and took a chunk out of Giuliana's ass. That makes them the first line of defense, so we grow those."

Distracted by hearing Romano, Kalinda lost her concentration. She found herself looking over at the man of her wet dreams. The week hadn't been total hell. He made sure to massage away every ache and pain and even gave her some more in the best of ways. For seven straight days she'd warmed his bed, and he slid into her soul.

Scarred inside and out, Romano found a way to smile at every moment, joke in the face of anger, and make her feel like her world wasn't completely on the upside-down curve.

He'd taken to also working with Zoey to grow a cage of defense around the pack land borders. In order to do that, they had to be pretty close. The open space, cleared for visibility against invaders, became their practice zone.

"Shit."

Kalinda refocused on Silva, who, while not screaming and withering on the ground in pain, was most definitely feeling something. Her cheeks were flushed, her thighs tense, and she shifted from one foot back to the other.

"Stop looking at him when we are training! Every damn time, you get all weepy between the legs and then you have to make me suffer for it."

"I am not!" Kalinda argued.

"Yeah, whatever. It's the only magic you've got that can push through."

They'd found out, with practice, that while Silva wasn't largely affected by Kalinda's magic as a Fae, she could still feel residuals depending on how much work Kalinda put into the power.

"It's because my sex healed her," Romano called out. "Do you know what this means? I've got magic sex."

Kalinda wanted to punch him and take back everything nice she'd said about how he made her feel good because, in two seconds, he'd ruined it.

"I am not going to tell you again that your sex is *not* magic."

"Kalinda, it's okay. We can let them in on our secret. Your magic really likes me … like … a lot. And it's fine. We all have addictions sometimes, and yours is just me."

She tried, unsuccessfully, to throw some serious pain his way, and her magic, the fickle horny bitch, immediately went for 'let's play ring-around-the-wolf-cock' instead.

Romano's answering growl only made her panties damp. She really hated that he was right. Whenever her magic was directed at him, all it did was leave her horny and him ready to give her everything she wanted.

While that was amazing, it was embarrassing.

"It's been a week, Silva. I can't do anything."

"Actually, you're wrong. You can make a Fae feel some of what you're doing, and that's no small feat. That's part of why we like being out here; the other wolves won't feel it," Silva argued.

Kalinda turned on Romano. "You said it was because of the Miracle Grow."

Zoey groaned. "I'm really tired of being called that. Can't we choose another name, like Tornado of Growth or Hurricane Power?"

Kalinda snorted. "Those aren't any better, Zoey. Just thought I'd mention it."

"Fine, take his side against the poor pregnant woman who can't even see her ankles."

Kalinda couldn't help but laugh, and it felt good. Zoey was nowhere near as big as she made it out to be. In fact, while she had a gentle swell to her stomach, one may not even notice she was pregnant if they didn't know better. But she was going to make the wolves around her know just how "miserable" she was and how they had to spoil little ol' her every chance she got.

Not today.

And besides, Kalinda knew what she was doing. "Don't change the subject. Why lie about coming out here for training?"

Zoey shrugged and mumbled something Kalinda had no chance of hearing.

"What was that?"

Yep, that wasn't any better when she murmured it again.

"Zoey, come on. Don't tell me you've gone scared after living here. What is it?"

"Fine. Every time you and Romano have sex, the whole pack has to get their freak on too. It's been really exhausting for everyone as a whole to be up screwing all night, so you coming out here is a break for them."

"Th— Wha— Oh my God!" This was *not* happening. "Zoey, you're lying."

Zoey cringed. "I wish I were. At least Dominic and I have gotten to know my pregnant hormones *really* well, so thanks for that."

"Are you telling me I've been turning the pack into one mass screw party?"

The smile on Romano's face made her want to punch him. His next words made her want to claw his eyes out. "I personally think it's awesome."

Of course, he would.

"No one asked you how you felt about it. It's all your fault."

His smile went wolfish—the only thing he was missing was the hanging tongue. "Don't be mad that you need me, baby. It happens to the best of us. You're not a bad girl because the old coots are getting frisky. Grandmas need love too."

Kalinda wanted the ground to open up and swallow her in one swoop. Now she understood all the weird looks and snickers behind hands when she walked by. She'd thought it was just because she was Romano's mate, and new, and … well, constantly threatening him with bodily harm because she didn't know how else to deal with him sometimes. Now she realized it was because they knew for a fact when she had him between her legs because everyone else got to enjoy the magic of the show too.

Maybe she should start charging a subscription for the service. Just ten dollars a month for Kalinda Kitty Kicks. The fact she imagined a name so quickly, one which also tied in with her branding for Kalinda's Katering, pissed her off even more.

"So you're sure it has nothing to do with practice of the Miracle Grow?"

To prove their point that, nope, it was about her magical share the love, Zoey and Romano gripped hands. Vegetation exploded around them, but it was different this time. Zoey used her free hand to direct growth, sending a path of pretty purple flowers growing to twice their size before she pulled them back to normal.

"We kind of got the hang of it a while ago. The day we got you out the Council mansion was the only time it flared so dangerously like that. As long as we're calm, I can feel where my magic wants to take me," Zoey explained.

Romano, the oaf, was still grinning like a damn loon. "It's all about the magical c—"

"Don't you say it," Kalinda warned.

"Magical c—"

"I said no."

"What? I was just going to say magical conflux."

She stared at him, really hard.

"But you're thinking about the other word, aren't you?"

She wanted to scream as much as she wanted to kiss him.

"All right, all right, jokes are over. It's time to get back to work," Silva ordered.

"I can't think like this. You can't expect me to focus. We're coming back tomorrow."

Things had calmed down since Romano and Dominic had returned from meeting with Arturo. Romano didn't tell Kalinda much, but she knew they'd at least removed the Viscount Pride as a threat and knew why the bastards had targeted her. She felt much better for that ... barely.

It didn't change the fact they were no closer to finding out how to get her from under the Council's thumb with the death sentence, what her powers really could be, or figure if she'd turn fangy in a few weeks. Not that she wasn't afraid of the Trinity—potential death could really cramp a girl's style! She knew she could decide to save her life by simply joining. Turning into a wolf was still dicey business, one she was still pissed at Romano for, no matter how good his sex was. He may have helped with a temporary stay of execution, but he could have just compounded her issues.

Besides, would she be mage, shifter, or magifter. *That's soooo not cute to make up words, Kalinda.*

She snorted, tickled despite the seriousness of it. She didn't get a chance to laugh much in life, but since being around the Lombardi Pack, she had to admit things were changing. She wouldn't tell Romano that, of course. His head was big enough as it was—both of them.

"Hey, chick. This isn't the time to zone off. We've still go—"

"Silva!"

Kalinda couldn't make out what she was seeing. The world slowed, an eerie silence permeating the land, but with that silence came heightened senses. Silva blanched, her face slackening, her mouth wide open, and a ruby pearl of blood slipped between her lips. She took one step, then another before she crumpled to her knees.

Was that a firecracker?

She couldn't get her mind to work. A loud bang. Romano's roar, Silva jerking to the side, Zoey's scream.

Would you shut up for a moment, I'm thinking!

But it didn't work. Not her normal sense of calm. Not the rapid-fire way Kalinda had become accustomed to dealing with any situation. Nothing.

"Kalinda!"

She blinked, stuck, unable to comprehend. Romano reached for her, even as he pushed Zoey to the ground, attempting to cover his Alpha's mate even as he gripped Kalinda's wrist.

No. Silva.

Kalinda ripped from Romano's grip, power seething, bubbling, burning her insides. Her heart thudded loudly in her ears, each thump echoing within her blood. *Silva.* Kalinda ignored everything else but her prone friend, lying in a pool of rapidly spreading blood.

The metallic tang of it was sharp in the air, making Kalinda dizzy. Warm, slick fluid covered her hands, but she didn't care.

All that mattered was Silva. She pulled her friend to her chest, struggling against Silva's heavy weight as she flopped, fighting to keep her head clear.

No. No. Nonononononono! Help me, please.

Kalinda reached inside for the darkness, the fires burning deep inside she knew she wasn't strong enough to contain. She pulled at them greedily.

"Kalinda, let me see her. I can't help if you don't let her go."

Kalinda whipped her head around, coming face to face with an uncommonly serious Giuliana. "Heal her."

She didn't know how her voice sounded so deep, so multiplied, but it raked over the wolf, pushing Giuliana to her knees. Pale and wide-eyed, Giuliana reached for Silva.

"You have to let me in. I promise I won't hurt her."

"You do, you die."

It was a promise from deep within Kalinda. Everyone, no matter who they were, was a threat right now. She'd do anything to save Silva, who'd been by her side, who'd fought to protect her and teach her to help herself. Who'd handled Kalinda's Katering like it was her own when Kalinda hadn't been there.

Soul deep, Kalinda knew Silva was too important. Her blood sang with the knowledge. She only let Giuliana move Silva so far, keeping their hands connected. The healer wolf worked fast, feeling her way past a gaping hole in Silva's back.

"She's been shot with an iron bullet."

Zoey sucked in a deep breath. "Did it puncture her heart?"

"What does iron do to a Fae?" Kalinda interrupted. She needed to understand. Needed to save her friend.

"Iron is poisonous to the Fae, like mercury to a human. It takes a large amount to kill them, unless injected directly into the heart. Even then, if dealt with fast enough, it can be survived. But the projectile has been spelled. I can't pull it out of her. We need Zahara, and quick."

"Save her," Kalinda demanded.

"I … I can't. Zahara is the quickest way, but that may be too late, Kalinda. I'm sorry."

"I'm calling her now. The alarm has been raised, and scenters are out looking for the shooter. Giuliana, do what you can."

Kalinda ignored Romano's voice. She didn't want his soothing. She didn't want him to hold her and make everything all right. She wanted to destroy.

Every. Thing.

"Kalinda?"

No. Not anymore. She refused to let someone die. She refused to lose someone else because of magic and the bullshit it created. She'd lost enough, and she wasn't going to let it beat her anymore.

You get out here, or I'll rip you out of me. I swear before all things holy. You earn your fucking keep.

Disrespectful or not, Kalinda was going to get in command of the flames deep inside of her.

We're here, Ales. We're here, they finally answered.

Help me. Make me strong enough to heal her.

It won't—

I don't care!

So be it.

The world went dark, spinning around, mushing colors into one until they were nothing but haphazard slashes of black, so much like the Chaos Realm. A pale pink light threaded with glittering silver lines, no larger than a spec but great in intensity, hovered, fading fast. *Silva.* Kalinda gripped that light, cradling it against her chest.

Not yet, girly. Not fucking yet.

The sticky silver lines, like steel spiderwebs, clenched tighter, making it hard for Kalinda to touch the pink light directly.

Binding. The girl is bound.

I don't care what she is, Kalinda argued with the spirits inside her. *Break that shit.*

The Ales speaks and knows what she wants … finally.

Whatever that meant.

Keep hold of her. Don't let her go, they whispered.

Never, Kalinda promised.

She held on tighter, pulling for her magic, infusing it with green for healing. The ground wasn't as hard under her knees anymore, and sweet air buffeted her face. Kalinda didn't pay attention to any of it. Everything in her was focused on the light between her palms. She sent all the love and care she could, wrapping herself, Silva's body, and the pink light into the color of green.

The ancient flames inside Kalinda pushed out from her body, whipping around her and blowing her hair free of the tight bun she had during practice. Her dark strands flared in the maelstrom, power prisming out in a rainbow dance of colors.

I'm a lightshow, Silva. Come see.

Slowly, painstakingly so, each threat wrapped around the light where it fell and twisted around Kalinda's fingers before burning away to ash. With each one removed, Silva's light grew. Larger and larger, heavier and heavier. And with the growth came such overwhelming magic, Kalinda could barely hold on.

Freezing ice. That's what Silva's light became—so cold it burned. She was Kalinda's opposite; hard where Kalinda was soft. Ruthless where Kalinda was kind. It almost felt nothing like the woman she'd known, and yet there was laughter there too. Freedom contained under rules and rites she couldn't fight.

She felt like she was seeing Silva for the first time.

When the light grew too heavy, Kalinda forced it back into Silva's form, into the bloody cavity left by the bullet's vicious trajectory.

"Come on, Silva."

Silver dust exploded, blinding Kalinda for a moment before a very different Silva was in her arms. Kalinda blinked, sure she was imagining things.

"Silva?"

"Dude, I think I rock. Like … even more than I did before. Oh, and nice aerodynamics."

What?

Silva smiled and pointed down. Okay, so that was a very unladylike scream that came out of Kalinda's mouth when she realized they were hovering in the air—*way* up in the air. Skyscraper fucking high.

"What the hell?"

"Shhhh. It's okay. You brought me up here, and now I won't let you fall. See?"

Yeah, she saw her potential death. Not cool.

"Look, Kalinda."

Kalinda forced her gaze to her friend, who now sported a gorgeous set of black and silver wings like a butterfly. They were much larger, though, and bent at an odd angle when she flapped them so they appeared to almost be treading the air like water. Kalinda hugged her friend close.

"You scared the hell out of me" she forced out through her tears.

"Are you crying?"

"Only a little."

Delicate fingers pushed into Kalinda's hair, softly untangling knots as they went. "You saved my life, Kalinda. It's my job as your *cosantiór*, Princess."

"What does that mean, the word you just said? And did you call me a princess?"

"Your guard or protector, and yes, I did."

Kalinda pulled back and looked at Silva. "Where did that come from? What the hell are you talking about?"

"Oh, Kalinda, I remember everything. And we're *so* about to piss off the Trinity."

CHAPTER *FOURTEEN*

"**Y**ou were all mad like *whoa*, and then got on Giuliana like death to Sunday. Oh, and then you *flew*. You freaking flew, Kalinda, way up in the air."

Kalinda had to laugh as Zoey described what had happened. Not that it made a whole bunch of sense, but since Kalinda had been there, she figured out the particulars. Silva still sat beside her, her wings tucked away now. Silva said most of her kind could hide their wings in slits in their back when they needed to. It itched like hell, but they grew up practicing it, so they could take it. Oh, and she wasn't actually called Silva. Her name was Niamh Danaan of the Silver. "Silva" was the only thing she'd known when she woken up after being bound.

"We know what we saw, Zoey," Dominic said. He eyed Silva. "You're Fae royalty?"

Silva tucked her hair behind her ear before she straightened her back and held her head high. From the pose, Kalinda could see so much more than she'd noticed before. Silva's grace, her way of managing and delegating. She'd known how to do it all because of her position within the Fae Realm.

"Yes. To put it the quickest, I'm sort of the Queen of the Fae?"

"Sort of?!" Zoey screeched.

"Well, I am, but the position is one with stipulations. It's hard to explain it all, but basically, the Fae were created for two reasons:

to manage the fate of Earth and to walk beside the Old Ones. Over time, and due to the evolution of humans, we've taken a seat to the back, but we still are called in times of great need."

"Is that why your blood called you to me?" Kalinda mused.

"Yes, and no. Not just any Fae would come for you. Your line is of the eldest, and as such, the royals are your bound protectors. We cannot deny coming to your aid. It's a blood compact created so long ago the paperwork is farting dust now, but you get the picture."

"You don't sound much like an ancient queen," Romano said.

Silva rolled her eyes. "I've been living as a normal Fae, not remembering any of my old manners and teachings. The information is back, but the control isn't." She shrugged. "Don't think I mind it that much. I like me this way. Besides, I wasn't exactly the best queen."

"That's what led to you being bound?"

Leave it to Dominic to go for the information. The man had no interest in frills. They had been sitting in his living room since the "Kalinda Can Fly" incident, and the pack lands had been put on lockdown. They were still waiting on the scenters to get back with more information.

"I lost my sister, and this was my punishment. I was ... conceited and bloated with my power. No Ales had been around for so long, and we forgot what that felt like. I was too comfortable and wasn't paying attention, too into my own life and wealth. My sister paid the price."

"I'm so sorry." Kalinda grabbed her hand. "Losing someone is never easy."

"No. It's not."

For a moment, Silva's eyes were haunted before she blinked, clearing away the emotion. "For now, what matters is, I have a way to beat the Trinity."

"I'm all fucking ears," Dominic answered.

A knock at the door ended the conversation, and Romano moved to open the door. Pasquale, walked in. He'd been the best scenter for the Bianchi Pack before they'd joined the Lombardi Pack. Dominic had kept him in place after the changeover.

"Alpha, we found the culprits."

Romano gripped the door, the wood creaking under the force. "Who?"

His voice was more growl than sound, and it went straight to Kalinda's nether regions. God, he *was* hot.

"Three lion shifters. By scent, members of the Viscount Pride."

"Retaliation."

Romano spun at Arturo's voice. Behind him was Zahara. They came in together, Zahara's gaze scanning over Kalinda and Silva with a mysterious smile before it locked on to Dominic. Kalinda didn't know exactly how to describe that look. Craving? Sadness? A mixture of both? She glanced over at Zoey, but the Alpha mate was too busy looking at Pasquale.

Wonder what that's about ...

"Arturo," Dominic greeted.

"Dominic. The men they found are dead. It seems Kalinda's magic has some combat use as well."

Kalinda perked up at that. "Say what?"

"I could smell old magic all over them, and it was directive," Pasquale explained.

"She turned them against each other?" Romano whistled. "Good one, baby."

"Why would they be retaliating by shooting Silva?" That didn't make any sense. Yeah, they'd lost the chance to get Kalinda and Zoey, but that didn't mean they had to keep going with attacks.

The men looked uncomfortable for a minute before Zahara stepped forward. "Because Arturo tends to handle threats with death. Kill a family member and they are bound to want revenge."

"Kill a— What is she talking about?" Zoey's attention was completely on her mate.

"Viscount's brother, and he was supposed to get you and Kalinda in their arrangement with the Trinity, as I told you," Dominic offered.

"Yeah, but that doesn't explain— You killed the brother, didn't you?"

"I ordered it, actually," Arturo interrupted. "It is our way, Zoey. You may not agree, but it is the reason they needed Trinity backing to even think they could come for you. How we do things is why you are protected the way you are. You know as well as anyone that Encantado isn't a paradise, no matter how pretty some parts of it are."

"That doesn't mean it has to be like this," Zoey argued.

Kalinda shook her head at her friend. "Sometimes it does, Zoey. I saw that man and what his pride was willing to do to me. You didn't."

"But—"

"We risked war to break your best friend out of the Trinity's hold when they weren't ready to let her go. Did you think that would be done without any blood lost?" Dominic asked her.

It was a hard question, one Kalinda didn't like to know the answer to, but she understood. Zoey had always seen the bright side of things, the sweeter side of life. Even if she could understand death may be necessary, it wouldn't mean she had to accept it. Zoey went quiet, but Kalinda could see it sat uncomfortable with her.

"I just wish it didn't always have to be like this," she grumbled.

"Zoey, shifters are violent. It's as natural to us as breathing, but you haven't been faced with that every day. And we are mafia. I'm a Made Man, so are the other men standing here. We can't simply walk away from that life. We have thousands of people who rely on our protection and our willingness to do whatever is needed. At some point, you have to understand it because it won't change."

Romano stepped forward, no doubt wanting to change the topic and stop the pair from arguing. "Thank you, Zahara, for coming as quickly as you did. It seems we won't need your services, but I'll still pay."

Zahara shook her head. "Today is free."

"But since you're here. This would be a good time to ask. How did you get free from the Trinity?"

Zahara tensed, and for some reason, Kalinda didn't want to hear the answer. "It doesn't matter, Dom. We have Silva who knows of a way out for me."

"Because she let your mother die to save you," Arturo answered Dominic for Zahara.

One minute, Dominic was still. The next, he was leaping through the air, fangs bared and heading right for Zahara's throat. The mage jumped back, her fingers working in the air in front of her, and Dominic slammed into a warded wall before he could get to her.

"You bitch. You fucking *bitch*. I will kill you."

Romano rushed to Kalinda and Zoey's side, even as Silva was on her feet, wings flared and ready to battle.

"Calm!" Arturo roared.

Dominic fought the stronger Alpha's power, growling his displeasure, even as Romano, Giuliana, and Pasquale hit their knees.

"I said *calm*."

This order made the lesser wolves in the room groan, falling to the floor on their sides to get away from the force. The Alpha power may not have been directed at them, but the force of it still reached them. Silva made sure she was to the front of the women the wolves could no longer protect. Even Zoey sat down, her color pale as she gripped her stomach.

"Dominic, the baby!" Kalinda yelled. He could be hardheaded all he wanted, but his stubbornness was causing the pup in Zoey's belly to also react.

Instantly, he stopped, spinning around to check his wife. When he saw her pallor, he blanched. "I'm sorry."

"I know, love. I know."

"Hey, what about us?" Romano got out between coughs. His tone may have been jovial, but his eyes were sharp on Arturo.

Dominic didn't answer his Enforcer and instead turned back on Zahara. "Speak."

For a moment, she didn't. She just stared, seeing something in Dominic the others didn't. "You look just like her. Have her temper too. She never liked to be told what to do."

When Zahara spoke, she had tears in her eyes, and the pain in her face spoke to Kalinda. She knew that pain and understood what loss looked like. It had intimately changed her entire life. Recognizing it in Zahara made her move closer.

"She was family, wasn't she, Zahara? Your daughter?"

Zahara's answering cry and cringe away from the truth of it was answer enough. She fell to the floor, her sobs bursting through the room, her frame shaking with the force. Arturo was at her side, pulling her into his chest. It was the softest Kalinda had ever seen him be.

"Your … daughter?" Dominic repeated. He stumbled back, and Zoey was there, burying her face into his back and wrapping her arms around his waist. Her support steadied him.

It was Arturo who answered as Zahara wept. "The Trinity demanded one thing from Zahara in return for her freedom: the life of her line. She refused to let them have her family, and her daughter was all that was left, or so she thought. The Trinity attacked anyway, trying to force her hand, and Zahara had the power to save her daughter."

"But my daughter hadn't told me about you, Dominic. She was afraid I wouldn't accept your father—a human mobster she'd met on the edge of the portal, an illegal affair. She loved him, and he cared for you the best he could. You had some mage blood, but not enough to pick up in a scan," Zahara continued. "So I had to make a choice: save my daughter, or my grandson. For her, it was simple. It had to be you. I didn't have enough power for both of you, and she knew it. I let her die and gave you to Arturo to care for."

"Why?" Zoey asked for her husband, who still stood in a stupor.

"Because the Trinity would have killed Dominic too," Zahara explained, her words punctuated with tears. "I put a spell on Arturo to forget who the boy was. He only remembered he *had* to protect him. Benedict facilitated it for us. If I had known he'd one day come back to go after Arturo— It doesn't matter. He would have used what he knew about you against me to fight the Trinity."

"With his death, I remembered why I took you under my wing and allowed you to be bitten by a wolf," Arturo said grimly. "Your mage blood, diluted as it may have been, allowed you to be changed over. You were human enough to allow the change but mage enough to survive it. Mages, you see, can't be changed into shifters. We have kept that from them for a very long time and hyped up the no-shift potion."

Kalinda blinked. "I won't turn into a wolf?"

Arturo shook his head. "No. But we had to have you think you would, or the Trinity would have read that in your mind. There are very few of us who know this secret, to keep it safe. But you, Dominic, were a bridge, something that shouldn't have happened. They would have wanted to know why."

"You're my grandmother," Dominic finally said.

With Arturo's help, Zahara stood once more. "Yes." Everything in her wilted, the relief on her face palpable. "I've wanted to say that for so long. The Trinity succeeded, though not in the way they'd hoped. They assumed I had to live with the guilt of losing my family by not choosing them, and when I didn't run to them, they changed the rules for joining the Council. But they did take you away anyway. You were so close, and yet I couldn't do a thing. Not one single thing. Every time I saw you, my heart broke. I worked for you and put away every penny you ever paid me. It seems your child is going to be very rich."

The small joke broke the tension in the room, and finally Dominic stepped forward. It was hesitant, a child unsure of where to go, until he shook his head and moved purposefully, dragging Zahara into his arms.

"*Ciao, nonna.*"

Kalinda wasn't sure what he said, but the heartfelt emotion behind the words made even her teary-eyed. Zahara let him hold her for a few minutes, clinging tightly to his lapels with a white-knuckled grip.

"Well, explains why you have a year-round tan, my man," Romano joked.

Kalinda hit him, even as she laughed. "What is wrong with you?"

"What? It's true though."

"Oh, Romano. It seems we have some unfinished business." Dominic's eyes met Romano's over Zahara's head. "I seem to remember you trying to bite my grandmother."

Romano put his hands up in the air. "Okay, in all fairness, that was *before* I knew she was your *nonna*. And, to be honest, she doesn't look a day over thirty. You have to give me credit."

"Actually, he did bite me. I just healed it," Zahara added.

Romano grabbed his chest in mock surprise. "And you, Brutus?"

The room laughed, for a moment the levity of life filling the space instead of the death and fear of the last few weeks. Even Kalinda breathed a sigh of relief. Dominic had a grandmother, she wasn't going to turn into a wolf, and Silva had a plan to get her out of the Trinity death sentence. Score!

Speaking of which …

"Didn't you say you knew how we could win, Silva?"

The room turned to her. "Oh? *Now* we want to pay attention to royalty? It's like I've been a wall for the last twenty minutes. Nope, I think I'll make you wait until tomorrow for the answer." She stuck out her tongue to punctuate her threat.

"How old are you again?"

"Three hundred and seventy years young, if you must know."

Kalinda sputtered. If she'd been drinking, she would have choked. "Did you just say three hundred and seventy years *old*?"

"Young. I said young."

That was … wow. Kalinda knew shifters, with their rejuvenating powers, lived longer than humans. Mages could live longer too, if they weren't killed or something. Roughly about two times the length of a human lifespan. But the Fae, it seemed, could do much more.

"Perks of royalty. Regular Fae aren't exactly that lucky, but they have pretty good boosts too."

"It's like elves!" Zoey chimed in.

"As hot as I think Legolas is, um, no. The pointy ears thing was ours first. How rude."

"Silva, I need you to focus on me," Kalinda interjected. "Remember your lifesaver? Your Ales? I'd really like to know how you plan to save my turkey."

"Easy. Take over. Duh."

"Make this make sense, Silva. I'm not following you."

Silva tittered before she flicked her wings again. Pretty, silver dusting puffed into the air for a moment. "You're Vasilios blood, the tamer of shifters, the deciding seat on the *National* Council. Starting to clue you in now?"

"I'm starting to see why they didn't like you as a royal. Of course, I'm not getting a clue now, Tinker."

"Did you just call me Tinker? I told you I hated that."

"It's going to be your permanent name if you don't answer in complete thoughts."

Silva rolled her eyes. "As a deciding seat member, you could contact the National Council directly to take your seat. In fact, you could establish you home base within your *local* Council. Oh, and national members rule the local Councils, did I mention that? So tell them to bow down, bitches, there's a new sheriff in town."

Romano got his faculties under control first. "Are you saying Kalinda can not only accept the offer to join the Trinity, but in doing so run it and make the decisions she wants to?"

"Got it in one. Now, the National Council will want to verify you, which is simple since you are an Ales, and the Trinity can't deny they found you. They may even get in a bit of trouble for hiding you in the first place knowing these rules. Or you can bypass them altogether and call the National Council yourself for verification and installment. Personally, I'd walk in there like a boss, but they may try to get a little dirty, so having some extra backing might really help."

"It can't be that easy, right?" Kalinda was too afraid to believe it. Too afraid to hope this could be the end if they got their backing right. If it turned out any other way, they wouldn't have the chance to come up with another option.

"We can always verify. We can petition the National Council on the grounds of having an Ales within our pack and the need to know how to properly move forward," Dominic mused. "If we go to them that way, they are bound to at least want to check it out. We just have to make sure the Trinity doesn't get wind of things first."

"Did I mention she's royalty? Make sure you add that to your communication," Silva added.

"What? You said that before, when we were in the air," Kalinda remembered.

"Yes. Why else would a royal be your guard? Like for like. The Vasilios bloodline is mage royalty. As a member of your family, you're like a princess. May not come with a castle, but it at least should include a black Crystal card. Those things have no limits, did you know that?"

"Yes, I knew that. Always wanted one because, well, shopping, but …wait. I'm a princess?"

"Close your mouth, dear, or you'll catch flies."

"I think I've had enough for today," Kalinda argued. She couldn't comprehend it all.

Zahara and Dominic. Silva as Fae royalty. Her as mage royalty. It was all too much and coming out too fast. She needed a breather, a distraction. The world closed in, fast and hard, slamming into her chest.

"Kalinda?"

"Dominic, call who you have to call. I've got to get her out of here," Romano urged.

"Do what you have to do. We can take care of it from here."

She couldn't breathe. She was just Kalinda, owner of Kalinda's Katering and a simple mage. She didn't have things like royal guards and magical powers to kill men from a distance. She couldn't fly through the air when her magic was at its highest and bring people back to life.

She was just Kalinda. Just Kalinda.

"Hold on to me, baby. I'm here."

And as she wrapped her arms around Romano, taking his scent deep into her lungs, she figured she'd be okay with Kalinda also being Romano's mate. *That* she could handle. His body moved against hers, wind ripping through her hair as he raced from the house. The freedom of their sprint, the speed with which he took her away from reality, was tantalizing and amazing. For a few moments she could breathe, her chest not so tight, her mind not viciously swinging from one what-if to another.

No, under his touch she was just Kalinda, and she could live that way.

The rest of the world faded as he barreled them into his home, his house reverberating with the echo of the slammed door. The silence here was better than the noise in her head, the cracking fissure of panic spreading through her.

"Tonight, just let me take care of you."

She hadn't heard anything better in a very long time.

CHAPTER *FIFTEEN*

There were many things Kalinda hadn't had in her life. Marriage, children, a happy 75th birthday with her mother, true love that lasted a lifetime, and the trust of a partner to never hurt her. Even when she'd been with her fiancé, he had been smooth, supportive, and loving, but not passionate. Nothing about him made her lose her way or be left feeling like she'd been in a whirlwind, but she'd thought she could trust him to at least never change.

He had, of course, changed.

But with Romano, she wasn't sure how to put it into words. As she sat in his porcelain tub, flamelight from enough candles to be a fire hazard, hot magnolia-scented water lapping over her skin, and a multitude of rose petals in different colors floating over the surface, she couldn't describe just what she felt. He'd even helped her put her hair up into a messy bun at the top of her head. It might be knotted in the morning, but he'd done a good-enough job.

She didn't know how he'd orchestrated it all: rapid-fire orders into his phone against his ear as he got her breathing, undressed, a bath run, and then her in it. While she soaked, he never stopped from checking on her and making sure she was okay—all while he never mentioned why she'd been so panicked.

This man, this *wolf* and Made Man, who always carried a gun, could turn lethal at the drop of a dime and smile at the next, played maid simply because she needed it. Not because she asked. Not because she told him he should. But because he knew, before even she did, what she needed.

Romano was silent now, watching her soak in the water, his eyes flashing occasionally when he saw her nipple break through the water or when she looked his way. There was something oddly sensual about a silent man sitting fully clothed while she was completely exposed. Everything since he'd walked into her life was new. She couldn't blame it all on the chain of events. Romano was a living, breathing craving in her blood, and she didn't understand how she'd gotten addicted to him.

"Do you know what it means to have a mate?" His voice was low and deep, perfect in the darkened atmosphere. The low light cast shadows over his scarred face. He looked feral.

She swallowed. "I have a feeling you'll tell me."

He chuckled, and she swore it was between her legs the way it rolled over her. The man was dangerous, that was for sure.

"I suppose I should have asked if you know what it means to have *me* as a mate, but you would have taken that to be cocky."

She'd give him that. "Romano, you're always cocky."

"Not with you."

She arched a brow. "Since when?"

"Since the moment I laid eyes on you. I told you about my mother. I grew up with the stigma of a child of a broken mated pair. It was unheard of for the pack. Something had to be messed up inside of me too, right?"

"They can't blame your parents on you, Romano."

He shook his head with a sad smile. "Oh, but they can. And they did. I was strong, one of the warrior class, and it meant women threw themselves at me, but it was understood it was only until their mates came along. To be honest, I didn't know how to handle women for most of my life when it wasn't about sex. I had a mother who'd run, a father left destroyed, and me, only prized for my claws and my cock. When Dominic came around, well, I found another ostracized wolf who understood me. He asked no questions, didn't care that people avoided us, and didn't look twice to pull me out of the Chaos Realm when others would have left me there."

Kalinda stayed silent, too afraid of breaking his story to her. What a sad way to grow up. Sure, she wanted to scratch the eyes out of every woman who'd come before her, but his hurt was so much louder. His treatment at their hands. The way they'd hurt him simply because they could.

It didn't make her exactly pleased with the women of the pack. Romano was a man to be respected. Despite how she fought him and argued against him, he never walked away, never turned his back. She wanted to hate him for claiming her, but she could admit his claim on her helped give them the time they needed to make some sort of plan. And could she regret they'd gone after the Viscount Pride the way they did after knowing what they'd planned? No, she couldn't. Romano, for lack of a better phrase, had put up with her petulant child shit and with an understanding she wasn't sure she was worthy of.

And now he sat here, pouring out his heart, his pain.

"I'm sorry," she whispered.

"I'm not. It all taught me something. I learned from them and Dominic to cherish what I was given. To protect it, no matter what happened. The things given to me are few and far between, but I refuse to lose them."

When he said the last bit, his hot gaze raked over her face, sending shivers down her spine and gooseflesh over her arms.

"To have me as a mate, Kalinda, means I will never walk away. I never thought I'd find a mate. Never thought I'd have a family. Dominic. Zoey. Giuliana. Arturo. You. I would die for you. Do you understand that?"

He meant it. Kalinda sucked in a deep breath. "There's been so much, Romano. I'm not saying I'm running away. I'm saying I'm still getting used to having someone in my life, and I don't know how to deal with it. I don't know how to be in a relationship when I expect to be left behind."

"Kalinda …"

She shivered, the water suddenly not as hot as just a few moments before. Romano was the fucking sun, blazing in the corner of the bathroom, rivaling any heat in the space.

Slowly he slipped his hand into his pocket and grimaced. When he pulled out his fist, he hissed, his face going taut and hard.

"What are you doing?"

"Do you know the one thing the humans got right about werewolves? Silver. Shifters hate the shit. It's like iron to the Fae."

He held out his closed fist toward her before slowly turning it over until his palm was open. She watched, not sure what he was doing, until he unfurled his fingers. In the center of his smoking palm was a shiny, silver bullet, intricate scrolling patterns on the side making it look like a flower ready to be opened. A hole had been drilled through one side, and a delicate chain had been threaded through it.

"To be honest, I cut myself before putting this in my hand. The burning you see is the silver's reaction to my blood. We can touch silver, but it's poisonous to us when inside our body."

Even as she watched, his palm stopped smoking, and she figured the wound he'd given himself had healed.

"Why are you holding a silver bullet on a chain?"

He stood slowly and came toward her. "Because I'm making sure you understand you have my life in your hands, Kalinda. As my mate, there is no one else who could ever make me so weak, could ever break me, or could ever ruin me the way you can. I'm giving you the power my father gave to my mother, knowing you could do the same she did. You're not a wolf. You don't have the battle of mating like she had, and she was able to break free. You could much more easily walk away. I know that, and I'm still giving it to you."

He slipped the necklace around her neck before returning to his seat in the corner of the room. Kalinda fiddled with the silver where it rested just in the space between her breasts.

"Romano?"

"You have the power, Kalinda. I know what that means to you."

She blinked, fighting against allowing tears to fall. An ache in her throat signaled she might lose that battle. This man slayed her. Not with demands or orders. Not with control or guilt. No, with simple and open honesty as clear as his jokes. He handed her the world because he wanted, for once, to have someone not turn him away. To have someone make him feel like he was enough.

And he'd been fighting for her, even when she'd made him feel unwanted just like everybody else. She was ashamed with herself. She'd been no better. Not understanding his story or what he offered. Not even wanting to see what it meant for him to have a mate who'd made it clear she'd rather fight him than let him in, and he'd still never let her down.

How exactly did you thank a man for that? How could she ever make him feel he was more than enough when all she'd ever done was take from him what he'd offered? She bowed her head, uncomfortable with her view of herself. She'd always prided herself on knowing just who she was, moving to her own rhythm and pushing on to be who she wanted to be. Instead, somewhere along the line, she'd become jaded and judgmental, hiding behind actions so much like others had done when they'd hurt her.

It wasn't often Kalinda could admit she got a wakeup call and had to smell the roses.

And she never wanted to feel like this again.

She raised her head, her gaze locked on her mate. *Her* mate. One she'd never claimed, except in her mind. She'd hidden behind his shield, but unlike Zoey, she hadn't stood and braced him when the world sent him shit. Kalinda wouldn't let it be like that anymore.

She stood from the bath, warm water sluicing down her form, and she loved how his gaze heated. How he followed the rivulets down her skin, taking in all of her. Her breasts were heavy, nipples hard in the cooler air. She stood before her mate naked, open, and exposed. She wondered how she looked to him as she stretched her arms high above her head and arched her back, the silver necklace bright against her dark skin.

Did she look dangerous too?

Romano moved to stand, and she shook her head. Now was *his* time. He settled back, and the look of confusion nearly broke her heart. She'd never noticed how he was always *doing* something, caring for people, working.

Cautiously, she stepped from the bath onto the mat next to it and reached for her towel to dry off. The whole time she kept her gaze on him. His fists clenched at his side and a muscle worked in his jaw. She liked that. Liked that she could bring him to the edge of his control just by watching her.

Once she was dry, she dropped the towel and held out her hand. Slowly, he stood and came close enough to put his hand in hers.

"Kalinda?"

She only smiled before turning and leading him from the bathroom. He followed her silently. It amazed her how a man so large could make no sound when he moved. How he'd honed his body to be a weapon when he needed to be. She had a better understanding of what it meant to be of the warrior class.

It was only a short walk to his bedroom, but by time they reached his door, she was panting. She wasn't sure who wanted this more, him or her. She opened the door and led him through before stopping long enough to close the door behind him.

His room was much darker, no help of the candles to illuminate, but the large windows with sheer curtains allowed the moonlight in. She could at least be happy his home was surrounded by forest. No peeping neighbors.

Once they made it to the foot of his bed, she pulled him until he stood in front of her. That same, sadly confused look marred his features. Instead of talking, she decided to show him. Spearing his thick, cool strands, she glided her hands through his hair, loving the way he moved into her touch, bowing slightly so she could reach.

This man. God, he warmed her from the inside out. Even as her fingertips traced over his face—the scarred left side and the perfect right—she couldn't ignore the precarious edge of insecurity and resilience. Fear and absolute control. He was a study in broken perfection. From his strong nose to his soft lips. The hard line of his jaw. The thick column of his neck. His broad shoulders, wide enough to carry a world he didn't have to.

And as she moved, she took off whatever clothing she reached.

Shirt gone, she could touch his chest. As she pushed away his restraining clothes, she skimmed his flesh with her lips. Kalinda used her tongue to trace over his right nipple, pulling a shocked gasp from Romano. She smiled against his hot skin before she continued downward. She kissed and tasted everywhere she could.

His belt came next, and she made sure to keep him focused on her mouth dancing over his abdomen as she removed it. He was hard against her hand, and for a moment, she was lost in the memory of him inside her. She would have him there soon enough, but she needed to bring him to his knees first.

Kalinda sank to her knees to be better able to reach him and mouthed his shaft through the fabric of his slacks. His thighs were solid under her hands, locked into place as he slid his legs wider to accommodate her.

Even in the restrictive control of his pants, he was too big for her to get her mouth around, his wide girth tantalizing. She wanted to taste him, to see how much of him she could swallow before she had to give up. Impatient and needy, she ripped at his slacks, yanking them down his legs when she got them open. She didn't even wait for him to get them off when his cock fell heavily against her cheek.

She licked her way to the head, taking in his musky scent, his power, and sucked the head into her mouth. He groaned above her, but she didn't stop there. She wasn't going to stop until she was good and ready. And as far as she was concerned, it had been too long since someone had shown him just how amazing he was.

Silken flesh, heavy weight, a definitive scent. Everything about Romano sent Kalinda's need higher. She wrapped her lips around his cock, sucking and hallowing out her cheeks, and slid as far down his shaft as she could.

It was hard going, even using her saliva to ease the way. He was so thick and long, nearly too much after just a few sucks. But Kalinda was nothing if not determined.

"It's okay, baby." He placed a soft hand on her head.

Oh, not even a little bit.

She was not going to let him do this. She wouldn't let him put someone else above him. Not tonight. She gripped his balls tightly, a warning, and he let her go.

"Okay, I got it."

Good.

Satisfied, Kalinda switched to a soft juggle of his balls, rolling them with her fingers as she worked him. After a few minutes, her jaw was warmed up, able to open up more, and she slid down another inch. Saliva dripped from her mouth, and she used her free hand to spread it over his shaft. Working with a twisting hand motion up and down where she couldn't reach with her mouth, she stimulated his cock, pushing her way lower on him with each pass.

Her throat rebelled, tightening and making her eyes water, but she didn't pull back. She let the him sit there, breathing slowly through her nose until the sensation settled. She had nearly three-quarters of him in. She could get the rest.

Bobbing faster, she worked him, her tongue dancing over his flesh and opening her throat wider. Slurping to suck in air, she pushed for the big one. Resistance met the head of his cock and then gave way, and she pressed her face to his groin.

"Holy. Fuck."

That's what I thought. Hmph.

Still playing with his sac, Kalinda swallowed around his cock, gargling for a moment to send sensations dancing over his flesh before pulling back. Taking another breath, she slid back down. It was a rhythm—down, gargle, slide back, breathe—but she found it, the swallowing of him over and over. He buried his hands in her hair, gripping the strands until they pulled over her scalp—hard pinpricks of pain and tightness—and he used his hands to guide her motions.

She allowed him, loving his pressure, the way he pumped his hips and made love to her mouth even as she pleasured him. She looked up his body as she sucked, watching as he tossed back his head and his muscles tensed.

Romano was beautiful. So beautiful.

Finally, she shook her head. He released her immediately, letting her take in her first full breath of air.

"Did I hurt you?"

She smiled. "I want you inside me when you finish. As much as I'd like to taste it, I need you."

His nostrils flared, and he went still.

When he reached for her, she shook her head and fingered her silver bullet. "My show, buddy. Take a seat."

His smile was wolfish, and she was sure she had one of her own to match.

CHAPTER *Sixteen*

Kalinda took the time to let him sit down, but that was all the time she let him have to breathe before she climbed onto his lap. His hands framed the globes of her ass, spreading the cheeks and squeezing them.

Man, was she happy for having way extra in that department.

She hovered over his cock, her arms wrapped around his neck, waiting to slide down.

Romano looked up at her. "You're killing me."

"Smalls."

"What?"

"You forgot 'Smalls.'"

"Who's Smalls?"

She laughed and shook her head. His sex brain was cute. She palmed his cheek. "My mate."

When he opened his mouth to respond, she slid down on his cock and kissed him instead of letting him answer. They groaned together as Romano stretched and filled her. Much like when she'd taken him in her mouth, she had to work her body down his turgid length. The man was big and, as cliché as it sounded, nearly too much for her to take.

But she worked her hips, rolling to take him easier. His hot mouth on hers helped, his tongue dueling with hers. With each pump of her hips, Romano pulled her down. By the time she was seated fully on him, his arms were around her back, clenching her against him. They moved as one, push and pull, up and down, wave after wave.

Kalinda's core clenched, pleasure spiraling deep inside her, ratcheting higher and higher. She cried out, losing her motion, but he took over. He jerked his hips up toward her, fast and hard. Each pound slapped loudly. Every glide deep inside her was hot and poignant. Deep and profound. She held on to him because she couldn't do anything else.

She ripped her mouth from his, trying to take back some control, to be able to move him where she wanted. It was supposed to be about him, and he'd taken over.

"Romano," she moaned, "let me."

"Love you."

"What?"

"You forgot 'love you' at the end of that."

"But—"

"It's okay. I'll love enough for both of us."

Shocked silent, Kalinda let Romano take over. Romano lifted them from the bed and rolled them over until she was under him. His strokes were sure and hard, fast and furious, sending too much pleasure streaming over her to even think of the revelations of the evening. She let him send them both over the edge, over and over, through the night.

The bastard was playing with her. He had to be.

For three days since the "he may have said he loved me, but maybe not" incident, Romano stayed busy. Oh, not so busy he didn't share breakfast, lunch, and dinner with Kalinda when he wasn't on patrol or on a job for Dominic. Silva stayed with them in the guestroom so she could be there to continue to train Kalinda while they waited to hear back from the National Council.

The days were busy, and the nights were hard and hot, but Romano never broached the subject of love again. Instead, he acted like he'd never said it. Of course, that only made her wonder more about it.

Not that she was in love. They hadn't been around each other long enough to feel that way—seriously!—but she still wanted to know *if* he'd said it. That was important, right? At least she'd thought it would be. But things were normal, oddly anticlimactic in the way things went. Zoey was flittering around being waited on by hand and foot. Giuliana was coming and going with her store and running it when she wasn't on site.

Kalinda's Katering, well, Silva seemed to have that running pretty well. What orders Kalinda had to fill, she cooked in Romano's kitchen and had full range of some of his soldiers to ship them for her.

Okay, so she could get totally used to having men running around with her precious baked goods, trying to be so careful it was nearly comical. And she wasn't sure if her threats or Romano's death glare made them do it. Whichever, it worked, and she was still happy to be doing something.

Still … had Romano said he loved her?

Ugh! This was starting to get ridiculous. Entirely ridiculous. Kalinda shook her head, hands deep in dough. All he had to do was freaking say it again if that's what he felt. How hard was that? Kalinda had opened the door for things to be different between them that night that started in the bathroom. They talked more, shared time just talking for hours, played and laughed. Hell, he even had her making jokes out loud.

He was *not* going to turn her whole damn life around and act like he hadn't.

I mean, I'm not in love with him, right?

She couldn't be. Okay, maybe a little. No, not even a bit. And that wasn't the point. He'd said something pretty damn important and then hadn't said it since.

Ugh. She couldn't really understand herself right now, and that pissed her off some more. It shouldn't be that hard to say what he felt and stand by it. He did it with everything else. Maybe he was waiting on her. Well, he could wait for a cold day in … *Sigh*. She was just talking herself into circles, and nothing was helping. He just needed to come out and freaking say it so she could go about her day.

"Uh, Kalinda? If you knead that dough any longer, it's going to pulverize. In fact, you're more beating it by now."

Kalinda stopped and looked down at the mess of dough she'd ruined. It would most definitely be fluffy bread now. She'd have to toss it out and start all over again.

"I'm fine, Silva," Kalinda retorted.

"I didn't ask."

"Have you gotten snarky after remembering you were royal?"

"Who, me? Of course not. I just say the stuff you wish you could. You're just jealous."

"I'm not jealous. I'm a princess, remember?"

"Yeah, but I'm a *queen.* I win. Boom!" Silva threw her hands in the air and cackled at her own joke.

Kalinda was tempted to throw the dough at her, and then decided being tempted was not enough. She picked up the dough, ready to belt Silva with it.

"If you throw that, I'll tell Romano you've been in here moping all day."

"I have not!"

"How many Raspberry Passions does The Daily Grind need?"

"They need Raspberry Passions?"

Silva rolled her eyes. "My point. That dough? It was supposed to be the Passions, but then you argued with me that they were bread treats and not pastries, so I left you alone."

"They're not even in the same class."

"I know. As I said, moping. So what's your deal?"

Kalinda sighed loudly. "I think Romano told me he loved me."

All laughter stopped and Silva's eyes grew wide. "You *think?*"

"I don't know. We had this weird moment, you know. Like … I said, 'Let me' and then he's like, 'love you.' And I'm like, 'what?' That's when he told me I forgot to say, 'love you,' but it was okay he was going to 'love enough for both of us.'"

Silva's face twisted with confusion. "What the hell does any of that mean?"

"Exactly!"

"No, I mean, you really are confused about that?"

"Huh?"

"Jesus, Kalinda. You run a business, have been moving to grow it globally, and can keep orders in your mind like a steel trap. And you are confused about this? Of course, he said he loved you, in the way you'd be able to take it."

"If you're so smart, why hasn't he said it again?"

"That's what your problem is." Silva gasped. "Oh my stars, you want him to say it again."

Did she? She didn't know. "It's not like I love him or anything. I just want to know if that's what he's trying to say."

"Okay, if you say so."

"What's that supposed to mean?"

"You're scared. The mighty Kalinda, the Ice Princess, is scared shitless her man loves her and she just might love him too."

"That doesn't make sense. I don't fear anything."

"I think you've had a lot to fear these last few weeks, a lot you can't control when you've been trying to."

"Are you calling me a control freak?"

"If the shoe fits …"

"You're just as bad as Zoey."

"Good. You need friends who aren't intimidated to tell you what's on their mind."

Kalinda shrugged. "Maybe you're right. Doesn't clarify this situation at all right now."

"Why don't you ask him?"

"Why would I?"

"Um, because you want to know. Look, men are stupid. He may not know you want him to say it. Or maybe he thinks he made you uncomfortable by saying in the first place and he's not saying it right now so he doesn't put pressure on you."

Silva had a point, and Kalinda could even see that knowing what she knew of Romano's personal story. Maybe he wasn't willing to put on her what he thought she wasn't ready for, and here he was again, making the decision to put her feelings before his. She could strangle the man. She thought they'd gotten past all that, but maybe they hadn't.

She tossed the overworked dough into the trash, making a note to take it out later that night, and decided she may have to take Silva up on her suggestion. She wasn't really on the team of waiting around to figure out. Not anymore. If that's how Romano felt, they'd deal with it, but he wasn't going to put that away for her. They were over that.

She untied her apron and headed toward the front door, already picking up her phone.

"Oh, Kalinda's on the warpath. I've got to see this."

Kalinda didn't try to stop Silva. There wasn't a point. The Fae was going to go anywhere she wanted, when she wanted. And when it came to Kalinda, she didn't deal well being away from her. They'd already found that out. They'd tested it, now that she was restored to her memories and powers. When she was more than a few miles away from Kalinda for more than a short period of time, she started to get antsy, and it could turn painful.

Silva trailed behind Kalinda as she called the one person she knew would tell her where Romano was without blinking.

It took a couple minutes, but Zoey answered with a breathless chuckle. "Hiya, Kal."

"I am not Superman. You know I hate that nickname."

"It's boss. I like it. I'm going to keep it."

"It's not for you to keep, Zoey."

"Yeah, yeah, yeah. Something about you loves it and that's it. Why did you call?"

Kalinda prayed for the strength to not kill her *friends*. "Do you know where Romano is?"

"As a matter of fact, I do. How about we trade my info for five banana nut bread loaves."

"Now I have to *pay* you?"

"The baby has to eat, and I'm totally shameless when it comes to food. I'll even give you the scoop as a deposit. Deal?"

How was she going to say no to that? "I don't really have a choice, do I?"

"Everyone learns so fast. He's right next to me."

"And where are you, Zoey?"

"That will be an extra pound cake."

"Zoey!"

"Deal?"

"I'm going to kill you the minute you have that baby. I swear."

"Threats will get you nowhere. I'm hanging up now."

Way to mess up a girl's steam. "Wait! Okay, one pound cake and five banana nut bread loaves."

Zoey squealed. "Awesome. He's about to leave and head home. He was just checking in with Dominic. Remember your promise. Loveyabye!"

She disconnected before Kalinda could threaten her with more bodily harm. Now she had baking to do when she hadn't even had to go anywhere. She really wanted to punch that girl. Seriously.

"Are we going somewhere?"

Kalinda looked over at Silva. "It seems the target is heading here. All we have to do is wait."

"Well, boo. You catch steam when you have to go get someone. Now you'll calm down by the time he gets here."

Kalinda wasn't so sure about that.

She'd messed up baking, couldn't remember her orders, and had been roped into making more. She figured she could use all that as fuel to stoke the fire. Not that she was pissed at him, of course. She just didn't want his habit of making things about everyone else to take root to the point she never knew how he felt.

She knew Romano could be in pain, depressed, or hurt, and he wouldn't tell her if he thought it would stress her out or worry her. Kalinda didn't want things to be like that. It wouldn't be fair for him to take all of her shit and then not be taking care of himself. He'd have to stand beside her while she challenged the Trinity, ran her business, and navigate the new world of her powers, all while maintaining what he did for his pack and the Family. They needed to share this, or it wouldn't work.

It didn't take much time for him to show up. He came in like he always did, his nostrils flaring as he scanned the house for scents, and then his gaze sought her. Kalinda smiled at him, deceptively hiding what was about to happen. He came to her, a ready smile on his lips, and took her in his arms to kiss her. Right before their lips touched, she figured it was as good a time as any.

"Do you love me?"

Silva, the minx, sat to the side, wide-eyed and unabashed in her attention of the conversation.

Adorably, Romano went red, the blush spanning up his neck and across his cheeks. "Where did that come from?"

"That isn't answering the question, mate."

He cleared his throat. "I'm not sure why you're asking."

He wouldn't meet her gaze now, and she didn't like it. She gripped his chin and turned his head. Considering his strength, it wasn't lost on her he could have ignored the pressure and kept his head to one side, so she appreciated he didn't do that to her.

"Does it matter?"

"Look—"

Before he could start some asinine excuse or dance around the topic, she spoke. "No more putting everyone first. You deserve it too, Romano. Let me do this, for once."

His smile was hot, filled with sexual promise and memories. She heated up just seeing it. "We could recreate that night, if you'd like."

"Including the 'love you'?"

He sighed. "You aren't going to let this go, are you?"

"Not a chance."

"What does it change, Kalinda? I could answer, and you and I both already know what I'd say. But will it make things different? Will it make you love me? You know, and that's all that matters. And maybe, one day, when you're ready, we'll be at a place we can talk about it."

Or. Not. He wasn't getting off that easily. Romano didn't know how to put himself first. She'd never truly realized how selfless he was, under the comedy and jovial personality, until recently. Even in the quiet moments, or when he was in protection mode, he was constantly thinking of other people and working that way.

She watched him for a moment and realized he believed what he was saying. He never expected anything he gave would be reciprocated. His relationship with everyone, even those who supported him and called him friend, made a part of him sit back and wait for it all to end, for it to just go away and he'd be alone—again.

How she hadn't realized how deep this went made her feel ignorant. Like she hadn't been paying enough attention when all the answers where there, right in front of her.

Kalinda shook her head. "It would change everything, Romano."

"Why?"

"Because a woman usually likes to hear the man she loves, loves her too. Why else?"

She should have had a damn camera. The click and flash of one told her Silva must have had the same thought.

"Score! This is going up on SpellBook. That face is priceless!"

Kalinda would ask for a copy of that picture later, but for now, she kept her eyes on her mate. Jaw slack, mouth hanging open, and eyes wide, she figured he was in shock. He'd even dropped his arms to his side, and she was sure if she blew, he'd fall right over.

"Romano?"

"Say that again."

She smiled. This was new—this connection, this release. Romano didn't let her hide away, and she was going to be the woman he saw when he looked at her. Letting her past and the hurt control so much of her life was over. She wanted to live here, in the now.

"I don't need to. I love you, Romano."

He closed his eyes, and his body shook from his shoulders all the way down. Pressing her hand to his chest, she felt his pounding heart under her fingers. She let him have this moment and curled into his chest, breathing him in.

How they'd gotten here from him threatening to eat her—in a much less sexy way to begin with—to now where she couldn't imagine her life without him, wasn't something most would understand. Maybe it was the life-and-death situations, or the mating call she may not have felt like he did but was intimately aware of. Maybe it was her magic, or maybe it was just a man and a woman finding each other in the storm and their messy pieces fitting together.

Whatever they were, here they stood, in his kitchen, a place that now felt like hers. She hadn't seen her own home in what seemed like forever, and she realized she didn't miss it as much as she'd thought.

And that was perfectly fine for her.

"I love you too."

To hear it did more to her than she thought it would. Suddenly, she wasn't a fan of their audience at all. There were some very fun things they could do on the island if Silva wasn't sitting there.

"I think that must be my cue to leave. Don't think you guys would like me to put up amateur video. *Although* it would really make some money if you'd like to. I've got a few sites we could use if you're interested."

"Get out, Silva," Kalinda ordered.

"Just let me set up my tripod. I can direct this and get the money shots. I promise you won't regret it."

"Out!"

"Okay, okay. But don't come crying to me when you're broke and your boobies are hanging to your feet. No one will want to pay to see those then. Well, maybe Romano, but you're giving it to him for free. What a waste."

"Can I eat her?"

"If you threaten to eat another woman again, Romano, I'm going to take your balls."

"I like when you get feisty like that."

"Like is such a boring word."

"Agreed. I *love* when you get feisty like that."

"Good. Now get me messy on the table."

"Your wish is my command."

CHAPTER *Seventeen*

Romano couldn't deny he was perfectly happy standing in the background as his mate got dressed for her meeting with the Trinity. Just two days shy of her deadline, she'd received word from the National Council, and it was going to make the Trinity piss their pants.

He'd spent a ridiculous amount of money having a dress tailored and created just for her to wear to this meeting. The sleek, white lines were brilliant, in some cut he didn't understand, but he liked the finished product. It was long-sleeved, framed her body like a second skin, and flared a bit at the bottom. She had on white heels with red bottoms that made him want to rip the dress off and fuck her right where she stood. Kalinda looked amazing, regal, beautiful. She wore three-carat diamond studs in each of her earlobes. The mate ring, a black band with two howling wolves facing one another with rubies for eyes, adorned her left ring finger. The ownership he felt seeing it there swelled his chest.

It was the only jewelry she wore on her hands, in deference to him. He loved that even more.

"Ready?"

Kalinda slicked her hair over her high bun, smoothing every imaginary hair into place before she lifted her head. The curve of her neck made his mouth water. The mark he'd given her stood starkly against the white of her dress.

"This is really it," she answered instead.

"You don't have to be afraid."

"I don't think I'm afraid, really. I don't know how to explain it, but I don't know what I'm going to do. I don't want to stand at the top, but I won't have a choice if I want to have any control over my life."

"Sometimes, those who don't want it the most are the ones who get it. You didn't ask for any of this to happen to you, but it did. And maybe you have a chance to do things in a much better way. The Council in Encantado has been running rampant with corruption and turning a blind eye to most of what occurs. Stepping in under extraneous circumstances can only help them out."

"I never wanted to do more than live my life and feed people delicious food, Romano. I'm not in the business of politics."

"Then don't make it politics. It doesn't have to be that way; *they've* made it that way. The governing body of the Council is supposed to oversee interrelations and help mages find their place. Does Encantado look anything like it's marketed to the outside world? You think the Family got a foothold here because it was just some easy mark with all the magic and power? We came here because we needed to be here. We came into power because no one else would protect those weaker and they needed some sort of help."

"You make the mafia sound like choir boys, and we know they aren't."

"No, but we were just as vicious as the enemies those people faced. We are able to fight the battles they can't, and if that means we have to take some of the pie to afford that, so be it."

Kalinda sighed. "I just don't know, Romano. I thought I had it all figured out, you know? Run in there, verbally smack them around, and storm out, but the more I think about it, the more I realize I don't know what I'm doing anymore."

"You're taking control, and sometimes that means not knowing where to go. It's not like you're expected to walk into this knowing what to do and just having to waive your hands to make it right. You may make mistakes, and that's okay. I'll be right there behind you. And Silva will annoyingly be there too."

Kalinda chuckled. It was a small one, but Romano would take it. He didn't want to see her questioning herself or wondering what she was supposed to do. All she had to take were the steps to put her in the position to do more. He knew, with her strength and control, she'd fit in and make her way.

"Kalinda, you're not just some nobody. You're a business owner, smart as a whip, and the woman I love who's found a way to snatch me from all my fear and give me a place by your side. That's not something easy. You fight for what you believe in, and I think you're worth fighting for. You've always been worth it. And now, it's your turn to fight for it, to fight for an Encantado you believe in. To make it a place where mage-bloods who are forced into its borders can find a place to rebuild and call home, like you had to. You can make it easier for them."

"You sure you were never interested in having a career in politics? You talk like a slick one."

"I'm only telling the truth. You don't have to have all the answers; you just have to be willing to find them."

She sighed, running her hands down her dress. He was distracted again, watching her. The woman could make a saint want to give up everything he'd ever believed in just to touch her. Romano couldn't deny that being with Kalinda had changed his life in ways he hadn't been prepared for.

He was more confident, moved with more assurance because he knew, without a doubt, he was loved. That someone had chosen him, despite all the reasons in their head not too. Because she'd fought against her past and hadn't let it run her off.

"You can do this, baby. I know you can."

"Eventually, I'm going to have to start acting like my old self, huh?"

"As long as that doesn't include walking away from me or trying to fight me all over the place, I'm good with that."

"No, I don't think that's possible anymore. You'd remind me pretty quick if I started to."

"Damn right. Just take the leap."

She smiled, a soft bloom of pride and acceptance. "Yes, I'm ready."

"Hell yeah."

Romano took her hand in his and escorted her out of his room to where Silva waited. If Kalinda was pure ice and appeal, Silva went for sultry command. Her dress was a vibrant red, matching the hints in her wings. *Whoa, they must be like mood rings or something.* It was flowy and hinted at exposed skin when she moved.

The two women were magnificent. Of course, he was partial to his mate who looked over Silva with a critical eye.

"Can't upstage me, Queen."

"It's your show, but we have to make sure we show up in style. Your man looks good too."

Romano shrugged. He knew how to make a power play through the visual. He'd gone for a black on black suit to compliment Kalinda. His guns were firmly in his under-arm holsters. This time, he wouldn't be putting them to the side when they entered the Council grounds.

They left, meeting Giuliana in front, and rode to go get Dominic. The *Capo di tutti Capi* had come prepared with a small cadre of soldiers. They piled into cars behind the main vehicle, and at the gate, Arturo's lead car and his men met them.

This trip would go very differently than the first. They weren't interested in a show of openness and an extended olive branch. Everyone here had battle skills and was prepared to use them. Zoey remained behind, in the event things got uncomfortable.

"Subdue and then control. It's the best way to go in," Dominic explained. "The National Council agreed to not alert the Trinity of our arrival and why we're coming because of how the Ales was treated, so there is no telling how they'll react. We may have their letter and stamp of approval, but we have to get them to see it in the first place."

"I have a plan for that one, actually," Kalinda offered.

Dominic looked to her. "What's that?"

"Silva and I kick ass and subdue."

"Come again?"

"They expect me to be weak, and if I use you to use brute force on them, they'll cry about being attacked by the shifters and call foul. But if *I* come in hard and fast, with backup, I have a right to. They disrespected me, threatened me with death, and maneuvered to have me under their control knowing what position I was actually meant to have. I plan to pay them back tenfold for that."

Dominic looked to Romano. "How much practice does she have with control?"

Silva answered instead. "At this point, if she's not careful, even I can feel the bite of it pretty strongly. I still am not affected the way you all are, unless I ingest her magic directly, but I'm protected from that because of my status as Fae royalty. A normal Fae would be knocked on her ass."

"There *are* drawbacks," Kalinda warned. "I'm not all-powerful. While I can take an Alpha or two down to their knees for a few seconds, the stronger the power I'm fighting against, the more it's possible I can be knocked out with its use. I can maintain against Silva at full power for about fifteen minutes before I'm knocked down with debilitating pain. It would probably be less time for a powerful shifter Alpha because of the difference in the magical quality."

"She's been a quick study with everything since the change in circumstance. They won't know what hit them," Silva agreed.

Dominic nodded. "If you believe you can, do it, but you have to get them under control within two minutes, or I take over. We won't risk them lashing out and harming those we're bringing with us."

"I can understand that, and I wouldn't want to risk anyone, but I need to do this. If I don't, I'll never know if I can stand up to them, and it will mean nothing."

Romano wouldn't allow Kalinda not to get her chance. She'd suffered enough at the hands of magic, and now she could take back her power and her life in one fell swoop. She may not know how she'd deal with the fallout, since no one knew how the Trinity would react—or if they would even bow down before they destroyed everyone.

If they did, Romano was sure the Council was going to look much different than they looked before she took them by storm. He personally couldn't wait to see what she did.

Several hours later, and all of them tired of waiting, they pulled to the large gate blocking their last few minutes up to their fate.

"State your purpose."

Kalinda rolled her eyes. "They really are all about pomp and circumstance," she muttered under her breath, but not quietly enough for the shifters not to hear it. They laughed, even as she answered the receiver on the gate.

"It's Kalinda Thorton."

The gates swung open without anything else being said. They pulled through, ready to face whatever came. The same over-the-top fountain and circular drive met them, but the landscaping had changed drastically. There were still the large, twisting rose vines and flowers Romano and Zoey had grown, though they'd been cut and manicured to look like they were meant to be there.

Romano looked on with a critical eye. "Looks like they found a way to turn our awesome Grow and Show to their pleasure."

"Grow and Show? Zoey will probably like that name a lot better than Miracle Grow," Dominic commented.

"In that case, I'm changing it back to Miracle Grow. I can't have her too spoiled, can I?"

"Since it's *my* job to spoil her, I suppose it doesn't matter," Dominic countered.

"Touché."

The cars came to a stop one after another in the circular drive, and the familiar lion's door waited for their entrance. As a group, they all got out. Kalinda and Silva, as planned, took up the front, Arturo and Dominic behind them, followed by Giuliana and Romano leading the soldiers. The level of firepower they had with them must have been enough to stop a small army, but Romano couldn't deny he liked these odds much better.

At the door, the Puss refused to open. "Leave your weapons behind, and only the Ales and her mate need enter," it warned.

"Yeah, not happening today," Silva warned.

Kalinda stepped back, and the others took their cue and did so as well. Romano watched curiously as Silva expanded her wings to their fullest, and they glowed brightly in the sunlight.

"Away!" she screamed.

The door blasted open, splintering and fracturing on itself, and the group rushed in. Inside the parlor, the darkness from the Chaos Realm tried to press in, pushing tight until Silva screamed, a painful cry of pure loss and rage.

"Silva!" Kalinda's cry was sharp and hard. "You bastards."

Romano didn't know how to explain what happened next. One minute they were stuck in oppressive darkness, all those who'd been touched by the Chaos Realm pressed down under the pressure, and the next, a blinding bright light cut through it all.

Kalinda stood at the center, brighter than the sun, and Silva was at her side, holding her hand. The Fae Queen and Kalinda were beacons walking them through the storm and leading them past the parlor's darkness.

"Are you okay, Silva?" she whispered.

Silva was pale and didn't answer.

They'd have to talk to her later, but for now, they had company.

Lennox, Yon, and Amalia stood at the top of the staircase watching Kalinda with varying degrees of surprise and need. Lennox, the bastard, looked fit to leap on her right then.

"You've come into your power, Ales. We are happy to see it. And you have a Fae at your side. It seems you've made your choice?" Amalia's voice may have been soothing and calm, but it still grated on Romano's nerves.

"I have," Kalinda answered. "Come down here."

Yon stood taller. "You do not command us, Ales. It is the other way around."

Kalinda smiled, and it went straight to Romano's cock. Strong, powerful, controlled. God, he loved that woman.

"You misunderstand me, but I'm kind. I'll ask once more. Come down here."

Lennox looked to Amalia who just shook her head. "I can't read her."

They were really going to have to learn they couldn't whisper around shifters. It seemed their power had gone to their heads no matter how long they'd been working around the likes of them.

Kalinda sighed, an exaggerated sound Romano tried his best to keep from laughing at. He knew what that sound meant, and every time he'd heard it, Kalinda got exactly what she wanted.

"So be it."

She stepped forward to the front of the group and focused on the Trinity. Yon was affected first, his ever-shifting visage stilling and jagged between two different faces. It was … creepy.

"That's not weird at all," Romano commented.

But he kept it quiet, only the shifters able to hear him. Yon stumbled, fighting the force holding him, and nearly fell down the stairs.

"Yon. Stop this," Lennox ordered.

It didn't change a thing. Amalia was next, screaming as she jerked forward. Kalinda never faltered, never made a step forward or moved an inch closer. She demanded they would come to her, and that's what she meant.

"I won't repeat myself again," she warned.

Her power whipped through the room, different and more insidious than the Alpha power, but not any weaker. Romano staggered under the pressure. Even being her mate, he couldn't withstand it. Dominic jerked, and Arturo grunted. Lennox couldn't take the pressure any longer. Within a few minutes, all three of the highest mages in Encantado had come to Kalinda's call.

Romano was so proud of her.

"That's my mate, by the way."

"Yeah," Dominic forced out. "We know."

"I'm not going to join Trinity." Kalinda stood tall, her backup behind her.

"Then you'll die," Lennox said with a hiss.

"Wrong. I'm going to *rule* you."

"You don't rule the Trinity; you are ruled by us. You are meant to be at our beck and call to manage the mage-bloods as we see fit. *That* is your place," Lennox argued.

"Tough shit I found out who I was, isn't it? I am Kalinda Thorton of the Vasilios bloodline, and it seems *you* were the one to misunderstand. I have an honorary place on the National Council, and, as such, have the right to rule the Trinity. That is the position of the Ales, didn't you know? Of course, you did, you lying shits. You never had the right to control me, and you never will."

Like the complete boss she was, Kalinda stepped right up into Amalia's face. "And the Fae beside me is Niamh Danaan of the Silver, as in *Queen* Niamh Danaan of the Silver."

"Bow down, bitches," Silva tossed out.

"Now, if you'd be so kind, I'd like to know where my office here is going to be. There are going to be changes around here, and fast. Encantado hasn't been taken care of nearly the way it should, and I might as well start reading up on the laws now. Oh, and here is the letter from the National Council, if you need it."

It probably wasn't necessary for Kalinda to push said letter right into Lennox's face and knock the man smooth over to the ground. It was even more crazy that she also stepped right over the stupefied mage like he wasn't there.

Romano was going to bend that woman over every surface he could at his home and the Council mansion the minute he got the chance.

Romano hurried to his woman's side, grabbing her arm when she wobbled a bit. Using her power against the three mages hadn't been easy, no matter how she'd made it look. She breathed a sigh of relief at his touch.

"Thank you."

"Always, Kalinda. I'll be here whenever you need."

EPILOGUE

Two months meant a lot of changes.

New onboarding for newly appointed residents of Encantado to help them find their way was well underway. A stimulus package provided funding for a time while they were looking for jobs to establish themselves. Kalinda had formulated a way for low-level mages to have apprenticeship programs under higher levels. If they chose not to, they would be hired under her company as couriers, by the Lombardi Pack Gardens Community Center, or within the Entertainment Zone.

Things weren't completely smoothed out, and there were still kinks to the actualization of her plans, but Encantado was firmly behind the new ruling member of the Council sitting at the top of the Trinity. Choosing not to live within the mansion but on pack lands with her mate meant people got to know her and what the Council actually stood for.

She was freaking *exhausted*. For all intents and purposes, her position was three-fourths mayor and one-fourth babysitting. But Romano made it all worthwhile. He never let her forget to stop to relax, make love, and remember she was just a woman who'd assumed a role instead of the role consuming her.

He worked with his pack and had his men help her when she needed. Silva stayed beside her and helped her with her decisions.

There was no better assistant, friend, or sister she could have. She couldn't deny things had worked out better than she'd ever known. Kalinda's Katering had gone global, thanks to the fact an Honorary National Council member owned it. She'd take it, no matter how it came. At this point, she figured she deserved it.

"Kalinda, where's Zoey?"

Kalinda spun around at Silva's frantic cry. "What's wrong? What happened?"

Silva still hadn't spoken about what she'd seen in the Chaos Realm that seemed to break something in her. She was still the same snarky Fae, but there was an underlying thread of pain to her Kalinda couldn't make go away. Now, every time something bad seemed to be happening, she worried if it was time for her to find out what happened.

"There's this kid at the door. He'd come looking for Romano, but he's not here. He says someone is missing."

Kalinda hurried to the door, not sure who had shown up, but if one of the pups were missing, there was no one better than Zoey to find them with her earth magic. But Dominic was zealous about making sure his mate conserved her energy as her pregnancy advanced.

Who she found at the door made her freeze. "*Lorenzo?*"

The once scrawny kid had begun to fill out, slowly, since working for the Lombardi Pack and making his girlfriend Cin's jewelry business a hot commodity. Right now, though, he was haggard, his clothes disheveled and his dark hair a mess like he'd run his fingers through it too much.

"What's wrong?"

"I don't know where Heath is."

"He's always with you. When's the last time you saw him?"

Kalinda was already moving, ushering Lorenzo through the door and into a chair at the kitchen table. While she waited for the young man to compose himself, she got him a glass of water and sent an S.O.S. text to Zoey with Lorenzo's name. Dominic would let her come for that, Kalinda was sure.

"It was a couple weeks ago. I mean, we're older now, and me being with Cin has been a bit hard on him. It was always the two of them, you know? Two orphans against the world. And then I met them and things … changed. I don't think he ever loved her or anything, or was interested in her in that way, but he didn't do well with things once we moved in and Cin got really busy with her business. Things were going to smooth out, I just knew it. But then …"

Lorenzo swallowed, and Kalinda hugged him to her chest. She didn't want him hurting, and she knew Andrea, his mother, would be worried sick about Heath too. She hadn't just adopted Cin into her life; she'd taken in Heath off the streets too and loved them both.

"Have you talked to your mom?"

He winced. "You know how she is, Kal."

She was going to kill Zoey for getting some of the kids and shifters to call her by that atrocious nickname. But she did know how Andrea could be. She'd lose her shit, and then things wouldn't be so easy. She'd have every parent in District 17 up in arms, posting flyers, going to news outlets, and trying everything she could to make as much noise as possible.

"But it might help."

"He doesn't want to be found. It's all my fault I didn't notice."

"Okay, Lorenzo. Do you know where he is? Know anything?"

Lorenzo looked up at her, tears in his eyes, and his shoulders curled. "He sent me a text. That's all."

"Can I see it?"

"Dominic isn't going to like it."

"I don't understand, Lorenzo. What is going on?"

Lorenzo dug in his pocket and pulled out his spell phone. After a few minutes of clicking, he turned it around so she could see the screen. It was only one short message, and then any return messages were denied.

> I'm sorry, man. Things just got too hot, and I don't want to do it anymore. I've been lying the whole time and I'm not who you think I am. If you're ever on the other side of my gun, know it's business, not personal.

No, Dominic was *not* going to be happy. No one threatened one of his, especially one important to Zoey. And leaving the Family after being accepted was not acceptable.

Of course, everything couldn't go right. Shit was going to hit the fan. And when her phone lit up and it was Dominic instead of Zoey, Kalinda was sure she was about to deliver the death knell.

DO YOU WANT MORE OF THE PORTAL CITY PROTECTORS?

Mated to the Capo:
Curvy earth witch meets dangerously sexy wolf.
Will Zoey accept Dominic's claim before it's too late?
https://books2read.com/MatedCapo

Mated to the Enforcer:
It seems like everyone in Encantado is out to get Kalinda.
Can Romano claim her in time?
https://books2read.com/MatedEnforcer

Mated to the Prince:
Pasquale is super sexy ... and Giuliana can't stand the sight of him.
Or can she?
https://books2read.com/MatedPrince

Fated to the Traitor:
Things are heating up in Encantado, and Heath is right in the
middle of it ... along with a mysterious Fae princess.
https://books2read.com/FatedTraitor

Mated to the Chaos:
Carlo has been lost for so long, but the past might hold the key to his future.
https://books2read.com/MatedChaos

Mated to the Moon:
Fabiana has struggled to figure out where she belongs, but Adonis is determined to help her find her place.
https://books2read.com/MatedMoon

MATED to the PRINCE

CHAPTER ONE

Giuliana Moretti paced back and forth in Kalinda's living room. Everything inside her was tensed, pulled so tight her bones ached with the strain. It didn't help her Alpha had clipped a leash on his anger only enough to keep the mages in the room from wailing in agony. She was ready to beg on the floor for him to let up the pressure from his power, but pride kept her from saying a thing.

Sometimes it *really* sucked being an Enforcer—a job she always thought she wanted until she got it.

Hindsight, they say, is twenty-twenty.

"On the other side of my gun ..." Dominic repeated the part from Heath's text to Lorenzo for the umpteenth time.

It didn't fail to make her wolf want to blast through her skin this time, as if she'd only heard it once. To threaten one of their people would normally be a death sentence.

But Heath ...

The Lombardi Pack had adopted Lorenzo and Heath, along with Lorenzo's girlfriend Cin, when Dominic mated Zoey. The young teens may not have been a part of the underworld side of things, but they were family. Heath had always been with Cin, and when Lorenzo joined the group, they'd been inseparable.

Sure, things had been a bit weird lately—understatement of the *world*—but all the changes around them would be hard for anyone. Maybe Heath had gotten himself into some trouble and that's why he'd sent that text. She didn't want to believe he was just another blow to them in the short time they'd been a pack.

Giuliana clenched her fists. "Alpha, he is young—"

Dominic whirled to face her, his teeth bared as his deep growl filled the room. "He threatened one of *mine*."

The worst thing anyone could do was to go against an Alpha like Dominic. He was a monster when it came to care for his pack, even when he'd only been *Capo* under Arturo in the Moretti Pack. Taking over the former Bianchi Pack and making it his own had only made him worse.

Not that Giuliana couldn't appreciate him for it. *But still ...* "Heath is one of ours."

Silence filled the room as Giuliana stood her ground. Alpha or not, she'd spent more of her life standing toe-to-toe with men like Dominic, and she wasn't going to stop now. He might knock her on her ass, but she'd make sure he'd feel it in the morning.

She'd always been one of them, yet different. The protected princess. The crazy one who snuck out at any time of night and wrecked fucking shop. Teetering between the two sides was enough to give her whiplash.

"Careful, Giuliana."

"*You* be careful. You don't keep me beside you because I kiss your ass."

No, he probably was keeping an eye out for her so she didn't get a hangnail. That's the only reason she'd been able to guess why Arturo had let Dominic take her into his pack in the first place.

Arturo Moretti, the Alpha of the Moretti Pack, didn't give up control lightly. She figured it had a lot more to do with her being a thorn in his side and wanting to pass it to Dominic than thinking it was because he saw her value.

Not that he didn't love her, but an Alpha male's love was ... stifling. Giuliana didn't know how Zoey dealt with Dominic regularly, and Kalinda ... well, she was lucky her mate wasn't an Alpha. But Romano was Dominic's number two, and if anyone could run the Lombardi Pack when he wasn't there, it was him.

Assholes. She could manage too, if they'd let her.

Dominic glared at Giuliana. "And I'm supposed to … what, ask him nicely why he said what he said?"

"Dom, you know these kids." Lorenzo's face twisted, and Giuliana rolled her eyes. "These *men*. They've been right by our sides and helping out through the Lombardi Community Center. They kept things looking pretty normal while we were all twisted up with Kalinda and the Trinity Council."

"And that's supposed to make me feel differently?"

"No, Alpha, it's supposed to make you think. What could send Heath running off like this?"

Instead of answering her, Dominic looked to Romano. "You have to stay at Kalinda's side. Her position as ruler of the Trinity Council is solidified, but she's got to have a chance to make the changes for Encantado. Zoey has a complication, so I'm here. I don't want to risk the baby letting her use her map magic."

Ohhhhh. You want my foot so far up your ass you won't be able to sit until the second coming.

Giuliana hated to be ignored.

Romano—mate to the newly appointed National Council member Kalinda—smiled. Of course, it wasn't a nice smile. Like, at all. Giuliana was certain Lorenzo was going to puke at the sight of it. Maybe he should, and Giuliana would make sure it landed squarely on said wolf's pretty little shoes.

The young man hunched in his seat and grew pale. "Are you … are you going to kill him?"

That was the twenty-million-dollar question, and Giuliana wasn't so sure Lorenzo wanted to hear the answer.

"If it comes to it."

No filter. No remorse. It was that simple for Dominic.

Giuliana also knew there was only one option for *who* could go. Dominic may be Alpha of the Lombardi Pack, whose numbers weren't as small as they led Encantado to believe, but he still kept those he trusted with internal shit close to the vest.

Before he even opened his mouth to say what she knew was coming, she sighed. "Think Arturo will let me borrow Ciro so I don't have to shut down my shop?"

Ciro was the best scenter for the Moretti Pack. The Lombardi and Moretti had joined in allegiance when Zoey's child was revealed to be a future female Alpha. Because of that, the packs had been helping each other with business the last few months. Ciro's nose also helped her get some prime products for her store, and she trusted him with the inner workings. At least with Ciro around to help her while she was working on this mission, she wouldn't have to stress about it.

Touch of Old—her vintage shop—wasn't about money for her. It was a place she could be herself without the regulations of rules and the walls of protection the men in her life were determined to build around her. Dominic gave her more freedom than her uncle Arturo ever had, but he still kept her close.

Being his Enforcer only meant she could fight for the pack when the time called for it, but he still looked to Romano for the most dangerous work. Mating had only shifted the way Dominic and Romano faced danger.

Or allowed Giuliana to be regarded as more than a healer when shit hit the fan.

"Ciro has already been called in and will be at your store within the hour."

A knock at the door stopped her retort. Probably a good thing because she would have made a scene. They could have at least *acted* like she had a fucking choice.

Hello, right here. Grown-ass woman.

She swore sometimes they were still in the 1600s when women couldn't make their own choices and live like they wanted. But whoever knocked was coming in, and her world shifted.

Mine.

Oh, hell *no. You sit your ass down somewhere.*

His scent hit her first—deep and cool, woods with a touch of snow, fresh game hiding in their dens. Nobody she'd ever met smelled like *him,* and her wolf wanted to roll around in it. Giuliana pressed her fingernails into her palm to clear her head.

Mine.

I said no, you slut.

Talking to her wolf like it was a person was a bad habit. She blamed it on a lifetime of having to befriend herself in a world where anyone could hurt her or betray the pack. Of course, that also made her wolf a hard-headed asshole.

And a repetitive one, apparently.

Mine!

Grrrr.

Everyone disappeared as Pasquale Bianchi came into the room. He stood tall, his head thrown back and shoulders broad enough to take on the world. His dark hair fell over his forehead and covered one eye before he pushed it away.

His body is a wet dream.

In solid black, the t-shirt stretched across his built chest, and his waist tapered into narrow lines where his shirt was tucked into his cargo pants.

"Alpha."

A single word. One that should have been in subjugation when addressing one higher than him. But somehow, Pasquale's call was on equal ground with Dominic. He didn't bend, and he didn't expose his throat.

Power.

She couldn't argue with her wolf on that point. The Bianchi Pack may have been no more, but it was alive within him. Her wolf did that annoying *yip!* of appreciation inside her head, and Giuliana wished she could strangle the beast. She was *not* in the mood for a chance to jump Pasquale's bones. Besides, the man had been driving her wolf fucking batty since he'd arrived on the scene, and Giuliana had been trying hard enough to ignore the rude animal.

I bet his cock is rude too.

Oh, I'm going to kill you, wolf. I swear to fuck.

Admit it … you thought of it.

She had, and she was more agitated than ever at her wolf's inner thoughts. But … the man *was* sexy.

Dominic's eyes narrowed, but he didn't reprimand Pasquale on his approach. "You will be with Giuliana. Your only goal is to bring Heath to me."

Excuse me?

Pasquale's gaze touched Giuliana, his nostrils flaring for a moment, and the heat of his attention raked over her body until her nipples hardened to painful peaks. He shook his head. "I can work better on my own. I've tracked Heath out of pack lands."

"I didn't ask. You will work with Giuliana."

Not that she wanted to work with Pasquale either, but what the hell did he mean he worked better alone? Giuliana may have been running a shop now, but she had been in the thick of things since she'd grown up at Arturo's side. Granted, she'd had to sneak out to do it, but who'd been there when Dominic was severely wounded in an explosion? Who got chunks taken out of her hide when they had to bust Kalinda out of the Trinity Council before she took over?

Giuliana, that's who.

Screw him and his high horse if he believed she wasn't good enough.

"The Alpha has demanded my presence."

Pasquale looked back at her, and everything inside her locked up and caught fire. His dark gaze was slow with its perusal of her body, from the top of her sun-kissed hair to the tips of her shit-kicker boots. She wasn't always dressed militant, but she'd been prepared to move on Dominic's order for Heath.

Pasquale's nostrils flared again, and he inhaled deeply, eyes flickering gold for a moment before settling back to bedroom sexcapade instantly. Ignoring Romano and Dominic, he stalked across the room to get up close and personal. His heated breath fanned over her shoulder, sending shock waves pulsing through her system. His lips danced just a hair from her ear, and she trembled.

Open floor and sink inside.

"I can smell your arousal from here, Enforcer. Don't push me on this. Neither of us want what this means."

His words were barely a whisper. Even with their shifter hearing, Dominic and Romano wouldn't have heard him, but she did. It cut. She wasn't sure why, and didn't want to examine it too closely either, but it forced her to suck in a pained breath.

Always, fucking always.

"Not today, Giuliana."

"Stay where it's safe."

"Just finish the paperwork."

"Heal the wolves."

"One day, I'll match you with a male worthy of you."

The last had come from Arturo—a promise of mating that would have enhanced the holding of the pack. She'd always understood that, while they looked like humans, they were wolves at heart—wild and uncontainable—with the added danger of mafia life. Their packs had been bred from Born and Made wolves who grew up in the life and never turned from it.

Giuliana's greatest asset was being a Born wolf with Arturo's blood in her veins. No one cared about her long-dead parents. No one cared about her healing skills. They didn't even care about her quick wit and fighting spirit. It had always been about what she could do.

It fucking sucked to think being with Dominic wouldn't be any different.

In some ways, the man raised as her brother hurt her just as much as everyone else. And now Pasquale added salt to the wound. Giuliana pressed her shoulders back, pushing her breasts against Pasquale's chest, and snarled at him.

"The desire for my wolf to fuck is biological, *Bianchi*. I go where my Alpha tells me to go."

She didn't give a shit about keeping her voice down. When Pasquale snarled, she caught the anger in his gaze before he could mask it. *Fuck. Him.* The Bianchi—more specifically their former Alpha Primo—had attempted to overthrow the Moretti Pack, and their inclusion under Dominic's pack had been a boon from Arturo when the dust settled.

"Are you both finished?"

Giuliana only held Pasquale's gaze a moment longer before looking at Dominic. "We are. We will coordinate and head out. All I ask is that I be given the chance to question Heath."

"Granted. But you'll bring him back here first. If *I* don't like the answers he gives you, I'll take care over."

She nodded. It was the best she was going to get out of him.

"Your place, or mine?" she tossed at Pasquale over her shoulder as she stalked toward the door. She was going to get this right, and she was going to put him in his place too.

"Yours."

His deep-timbred response nearly made her knees weak. It would have really messed her up her bad girl exit by falling out on the floor. Totally.

Mine!

Not if I can help it. I've got toys if this gets too hard for little old you.

I already know what I want to play with.
Ugh. You're an asshole.
He can play with that too.

Giuliana officially hated her wolf more than all the bastards in the room.

End of sample.
Click here

https://www.books2read.com/MatedPrince

to continue reading
Mated to the Prince.
Book 3 in the
Portal City Protectors series.

ABOUT THE *AUTHORS*

Georgette

Georgette St. Clair writes hot, sexy romances starring Alpha heroes. The road to love may be rocky and fraught with peril (and humor and scorchtastic sex and healthy heapings of snark), but her shifters will stop at nothing to claim the women they love.

Georgette has worn many hats in life: newspaper reporter, EMT, internet marketer, cocktail waitress, temp, nurse's aide (not in chronological order).

When she's not rescuing fur-babies, she spends her days in a fantasy universe where she nudges her smart-mouthed, take-no-gruff heroines onto paths which will set them on a collision course with true love.

FOLLOW GEORGETTE

Facebook
www.facebook.com/georgettewrites
Newsletter
georgettewrites.com/newsletter
Goodreads
smarturl.it/GR-Ginger
Website
georgettewrites.com

LeTeisha

Writing professionally since 2008, LeTeisha Newton's love of romance novels began long before it should have. After spending years sneaking reads from her grandmother's stash, she finally decided to pen her own tales. As many will do during their youth, she bounced from fantasy, urban literature, mainstream, interracial, paranormal, heterosexual, and LGBT works until she finally rested in contemporary romance.

LeTeisha is all about deep angst and angry heroes who take a bit more loving to smooth their rough edges. Love comes in many sizes, shapes, and colors, as well as with—or without—absolute beauty and fairy tale sweetness. She writes the darker tales because life is hard … but love is harder.

FOLLOW LETEISHA:

Facebook
smarturl.It/fb-leteisha

Website
smarturl.It/leteisha-website

Goodreads
smarturl.It/gr-leteisha

Newsletter
smarturl.It/lt-newsletter

Printed in Great Britain
by Amazon

37859353R00118